Ancient History Rediscovered

BY

K.J.Goss

Ancient History Rediscovered

ISBN Number: 978-0-9997533-8-5

To Marilyn,

a dear friend and faithful reader.

Introduction

A new adventure follows Eric Dexter as he again returns to the jungles of the Yucatan. He rejoins his Maya friends for further research into their almost forgotten history.

His previous two seasons there, as told in "The Dead Living Mummy" ignited in him a thirst for past history closer to home.

In "The Ancient Ones" he chose the American south west. His simple search for signs of early indigenous life spiraled into an exciting discovery of connections far and wide that could possibly rewrite history as we know it today.

An added bonus for Eric was finding love which had eluded him for so long, by choice mostly because of his work and ancient research. The peace and majesty of the desert opened up the pathway to unasked for romance in the form of a Navajo woman. Her twin names of Dove of Spring or Violet matched her Navajo bearing wonderfully as Eric fell under her spell.

Chapter 1

Eric Dexter followed the now familiar trail up from the river. The dugout canoe "Taxi" dropped him and his equipment off and instantly put off on the return to Oxtec. Common sense told him he should not be roaming the jungle alone and unarmed, but the excitement of being part of his symphonic jungle sounds again drove him fearlessly, though foolhardily on. He felt confident he was on the correct trail for two reasons: the GPS and the recent machete strokes on the tangled undergrowth. Eric guessed he was only three weeks behind his Mayan friends in returning to the lost city. The original trip here took almost three days, mainly because the jungle was virgin at that time with every step a struggle even with the slashing machetes. Eric convinced himself, if all went well, he could do it in just under two days.

"Oh, if I only had that vial of mysterious sand." I thought.

I forged on in good spirits knowing there was rest and safety at the trail's end. I pushed the daylight till I had just enough light to hang my hammock. Safe inside my mosquito netting I satisfied my hunger with an energy bar and settled back to my favorite night time symphony supplied by the many instruments of the musical jungle. Not the usual we see in a symphony hall, however making music just as sweet; the birds, bugs, winds and animals in a harmony never caught by notes on paper.

He whispered a soft good night to Dove of Spring, his beautiful Navajo love that he left behind on the desert of Colorado, falling off to sleep with a smile in his heart and on his face.

Screeching monkeys from high in the canopy were my alarm clock. It was barely sunrise but I excitedly packed up my hammock while munching on another energy bar. Double checking the GPS, I was on my way confident I would be at the lost city by night fall.

"I wonder if they named the settlement yet," he said aloud thinking of Frank Thurber and how they thought of possibly adding his name to it. After all it was his dream, his discovery and he worked hard to uncover its existence.

I set himself the best pace allowed by the jungle following the trail of the recent slash marks of the team from just a few weeks ago. I passed what I knew were excellent photo OPS choosing not to accept any delays. I knew there would be many more in the weeks ahead.

Comfortable with my progress, my confidence was growing as I recognized more and more familiar landmarks.

After four plus hours I decided on a short rest break and another energy bar. I had been sipping water during my trek but knew I still had plenty.

During the break my eyes never stopped scanning the surrounding area. Twice something clicked in my head. I knew from past experiences something was drawing me in. Another stele or stone structure covered with Mayan Glyph's perhaps. I was not sure but also did not want to interrupt my self imposed time schedule.

Making note of the GPS heading and continuing on my way at a faster than normal pace, or at least what ever the jungle would allow, I was feeling elated with my forward gain.

Eric knew he was doing well and did not allow his thoughts to wander to more pleasant distractions, such as Violet or Dove of Spring to use her Navajo name. There would be plenty of time for that once settled in at the base camp. He even amazed himself at sticking to his self imposed discipline.

I advanced another one hundred yards or so and then, almost like a sixth sense I felt I was being watched. I stopped, then moving extremely slow, I completed a three hundred and sixty degree circle, eyes searching. Back at my starting point not twenty yards away was one of the most beautiful cats I had ever seen. Instantly identifying it as a jaguar I froze in place. I quickly remembered Diego staring down the cat before.

"But that was just a dream," I told myself. "Oh well, what have I got to lose ? If I can talk to tarantulas, why not a large cat ?"

I quickly recalled the words of Whispering Wind, the wise Navajo elder, and his referencing of communicating with the Great Spirits other creatures.

Relaxing and showing no fear Eric let his mind reach out to the creature before him, hoping for a non verbal communication link. Thinking nothing but good intentions he remained still. In a little more than a minute he felt an unidentifiable sensation of chill run through his body. He maintained eye contact with the large challenger and softened his thoughts even more.

"I'm not here to hurt you in any way my friend. I just want to pass through your home land." I whispered softly with more emphasis on mind projection than actual voice contact. After a short stretch I again felt that chill sensation. I was positive it was a communication vibration. Some would call it wishful thinking but I actually believed this was possible.

The jaguar slowly assumed a sitting position. I followed suit, squatting down on my haunches. The standoff continued for many more minutes, there was no way of measuring. Then this jungle beauty, without rushing, yawned and slowly moved to all fours and strolled away in a direction ninety degrees to my chosen path.   Either my mind communication worked or this jungle beauty had already satisfied his appetite. I waited a good five minutes more before I also rose and continued my travels in the direction of the base camp moving at a slower pace trying, I hoped, to keep my mind clear of any aggressive thoughts.

I checked periodically behind me and was satisfied I was not being stalked. After another ten minutes I picked up my pace to make up for the lost time with the magnificent jungle creature. I dwelled on its natural beauty, thinking of man's injustice to nature by hunting them just for sport.

I also decided not to mention this little incident to my research friends. They will think I went the way of Frank and the losing my mind thing.

~ ~ ~ ~

Checking my watch I knew I could still make it before total darkness, but because of the thickness of the overhead canopy it was like traveling in the dusk hours all day.

Another forty minutes passed quickly and I knew I was there when I heard the distinct sounds I had grown accustomed to during two seasons of research. Listening carefully I could hear the welcome chatter of familiar voices, characteristic voices of my four valued friends. Speaking not too loudly so as not to startle them I made myself known by saying.

"So this is how you spend your time and money when you're supposed to be working. What will your backers say ?"

Surprised and happy the four friends rushed to meet Eric and relieve him of his burden.

"What the hell are you doing here ? Aren't you supposed to be in the desert. ? What did you do, make a wrong turn and get lost ?"

The hugs and back slapping finished I was escorted to the table. Some remnants of dinner were still visible which tugged at my own stomach alarms.

" And what the hell are you doing roaming the jungle alone. You don't even have a machete." asked Mario.

"I have a three inch pocket knife." I chided back.

Again looking at the dinner plates I asked.

"Is there anything left ? I am famished. These energy bars only go so far."

In no time at all a full plate was set before me which I wolfed down in between answering questions not daring to ask what it was. All agreed this was the way it was supposed to be, the five cooperatively working together. Diego spoke up about Dan.

"Too bad you couldn't talk Lone Buffalo in to joining us. That really would have been great."

"You're right." I agreed. "He also is a seasoned archeologist slash anthropologist and was of great help to me in the desert, or I should say we helped each other."

Relaxed now with a full stomach I proceeded to outline my last couple of months and what I uncovered. That part of my story, of course, caught every ones attention.

"If you think about it, that feathers nicely in with the gold room we discovered." Carlos stated.

"You're right." I answered . "That's the first thing I thought of when Dan and I uncovered the hidden chest. Speaking of hidden things, what have you done about the gold room ?"

"Absolutely nothing yet." volunteered Mateo. "We are still the only five who know of it."

Mario picked up the explanation from here.

"We wanted to further our research unobstructed by government interference before we turned over the city to the antiquities people. And to keep the treasure hunters away. They will just make a shambles of the place while destroying real history."

I went on to give a brief story of Professor Tallman and his selling of the documents.

Stories went back and forth for almost two more hours when I finally apologized and admitted I needed some sleep. All agreed with the sleep idea.

I automatically headed for my favorite spot that was home to me for the two seasons of the past. Diego accompanied me and helped string my hammock and mosquito netting. He then jokingly mentioned,

"It seems like I did the same thing a couple of years ago."

"And you taught me well also. This is one of those things I will never forget." I replied with a happy grin.

Alone now in my favorite corner of the jungle I relaxed and felt at home. I instantly tuned into my familiar night time symphony. Lost again in my tranquility, I zipped up my netting and settled back happy to be home. I silently said good night to Dove of Spring and allowed the serenade to take me away.

Chapter 2

After a wonderful night of sleep I was first one up alone at first light. I quietly made my way to the coffee pot preparing it the usual way. Comfortable at the table I looked around.

The camp was basically the same setup as the previous years. I reminisced a while thinking how much I actually enjoyed the search and discovery of the unknown. Not just the thrill of the chase but the education of history. There are those who do not like the idea of rewriting accepted history yet more changes show up every day, most of which have been lost or hidden before the public becomes aware of them. History is still history but we must accept new directions on old stories. It is hard to change ones beliefs, but that is what makes history so interesting. Finding artifacts is concrete living proof of things that took place in all the yesteryears past. They must be included in the story of the past even if that means some rewriting. We can learn great amounts about our future if we accept the facts of our past, but the establishment paradigm does not like the challenge of new discoveries especially if it means rewriting what they support as truths of the past.

"Enough philosophical discussions with yourself Eric, have some more coffee and decide what your plans are now that you are here."

The others had not stirred yet and I realized it was still very early. Looking at the main pyramid structure reminded me to pay my respects to the king and to Frank.

Coffee mug in hand Eric proceeded to the tomb.

Not that I expected it but nothing had changed. I did notice though a small wooden block with Glyph's set on top of the casket.

"Probably a prayer wish made by the others." he thought, realizing he would not even question it.

Frank's repository still set where they agreed. I whispered a few positive thoughts on behalf of Frank to whoever his God was. It wasn't much I knew, but Frank had been a longtime friend up to the very end when he slipped.

I sat on the bench I usually occupied and let my mind drift to the past couple of years. The excitement I felt on each discovery was a sensation that could not be discarded, nor did I want to. Being alone I spoke my thoughts out loud.

"I wonder what, if anything, I'll come across on this research season."

"Your efforts will not go unfulfilled my friend. New things will come to all chosen ones."

Eric, a half smile on his face comfortably answered.

"I was wondering when I would hear from you again. What have you got in store for me in this season of discovery ?"

"Ever the curious Eric. I see you have not changed. As always Eric you need not my assistance in the realm of discovery. Think not always vertical, horizontal is also a plane of discovery. I am pleased you are here my friend. There is much work yet to be accomplished."

"What kind of work are you referring to Atol ?"

I did not expect an answer nor did I receive one. I knew the king well enough by now to know the mind connection had been severed. Laughing to myself I voiced aloud.

"Riddles seem to be the king's one enjoyable pastime."

I then decided to return to the camp trying to unravel the horizontal hint and what it could mean.

Nearing the dining tent I saw Carlos just filling his coffee mug. Following his lead I refilled my own and joined him at the table.

"Just paying my respects to the king and Frank." I volunteered.

"I figured as much." replied Carlos. "I wouldn't expect anything less from a good Mayan."

A hint of pride ran through me knowing a statement like that from Carlos was sincere.

"So you found a connection of the Maya and Navajo in your desert adventure." stated a smiling Carlos. Noticing my quizzical look he added. "Mario and Diego filled me in on the funeral you planned. I was deeply touched by your caring."

I answered with "It was the only proper thing to do and the Navajo people were most caring and understanding. They wanted to be part of the joint funeral. They thought it only proper. You know "Joined in life; joined in death".

As a matter of fact I just remembered. Wait here" I directed Carlos. Returning to my chosen sleep area I dug into one of my packs, retrieving the scroll presented to me by Whispering Wind and Dove of Spring.

Back at the table Mateo and Mario had also joined us. I handed the scroll to Carlos.

"This and many more were part of our treasure yield." I stated.

Carlos with the help of Mario carefully unrolled the ancient document.

"This is definitely ancient Mayan." whispered Mario but loud enough for all to hear.

"Can you guys read it ?" I inquired hopefully.

"It might take a little time but I believe we can do it." replied an enthusiastic Carlos.

"I was hoping you would say that. The "Dineh", that's what the Navajo call themselves, were looking forward to positive results. This is just one of many such items. The Navajo are anxiously waiting anything to help further explain their past. They are truly anticipating a positive connection to their southern neighbors."

Eric then went on to layout in detail all they had discovered artifact wise but also emphasizing the trade contracts from around the world. The Navajo also were fiercely interested in sharing the results with the world of these efforts, though it meant rewriting the history books.

The four Maya scientists also agreed and right away spoke of joint presentations to the world openly proclaiming the validity of their Navajo and Mayan research.

Diego at last joined the others and after the usual ribbing for sleeping late, was brought up to date on the scroll. Thinking back to the day before, Diego asked for more detail about Eric's injuries.

"I'm all right now, but the first day or so after they found me I was hurting and was told I was out of my head for awhile."

"We knew that all along." interjected Mario.

"Thanks pal," I said before I continued. " Then their medicine man gave me something to drink, the taste of which I wouldn't wish on my worst enemy. I must admit though it was a miracle cure."

"That sounds like the same thing my grandfather forced on me when I was younger." said Mateo. "But you are right. It was an instant healer. I hope those secrets never disappear."

Eric sarcastically added.

"Let's hope they stay with families also and are not grabbed by some pharmaceutical combine just to make millions with."

The others, surprised at Eric's cynical comment, easily agreed.

Eric, to lighten the mood he created, asked about what they were planning for the day and how could he be of assistance.

His question was welcomed as they all spoke at once outlining their projects and how they could use his help.

"They have not cloned me yet so how about assigning me to where my few talents might possibly prove useful." quipped Eric.

Continuing the joking mood, Carlos threw out.

"Your main talent seems to be discovering hidden history no matter where you go, so we should let you choose who you want to work with. Who is up for a new discovery today raise your hand and you get Eric for the day. After that we will each get a turn with him."

All four were happy to take part in the joviality with Mario making a decision.

"To start with, since he got here late it should be up to him to make breakfast today."

It was unanimously decided as the four Maya friends sat back comfortably each sipping their coffee. I got the message and arose mumbling for all to hear.

"I could have stayed in the desert and had breakfast in bed."

"That's not a bad idea." chided Diego. "Could you serve me in my hammock ?"

~ ~ ~ ~ ~ ~

Breakfast over, the preparation of which was shared cooperatively, the days plans were discussed. The original four would continue their previous days projects allowing Eric the day to re-acquaint himself with all the facets of the ongoing research. In other words it was a free day for Eric to wander the area and catch up on the layout of the city as it stood today.

I volunteered to clean up after breakfast allowing the others to start their day. Being alone I let my mind drift to Violet, albeit for only a short time. I did miss her but accepted the decision I made.

With the kitchen secure and a fresh pot of coffee brewing I grabbed my camera and headed for the tomb.

I had no trouble remembering all the hidden doorways and soon found myself in the hallway of paintings. I stood comparing this art work with the painting found in the secret room in the desert. I reaffirmed to myself that it was definitely the same style if not the same artist. Diego's commission by Atol had been completed. The color and style were so much alike you would think this also was hundreds if not thousands of years old instead of just a year or two. No matter, I captured Diego's work on film to file with the others accompanied by the proper notations of course.

I continued out the hidden portal exiting to the surrounding jungle. Remembering the session of the demonstration of the scepter and its power, I headed for that area. Not having been used that much, nature had already started her reclamation of the space. As I stood there thinking of the magic sand, a small part of me wished I still had it, yet I was truly pleased with myself that it was gone. Who knows I may come across it again someday

I continued on to where the golden artifacts and treasure were secreted but chose not to enter alone remembering Frank's death fall.

My wanderings actually filled most of the day and found myself back at the kings tomb at the scroll library. I sat there for a while contemplating what history they would reveal when finally deciphered. Breaking my own nostalgia spell I realized I spent most of the day non - productively. Feeling slightly guilty I made my way back to the kitchen area deciding to throw dinner together depending on what I could find.

"This is the least I can do for the guys since I goofed off all day." I thought.

I managed to put together rice and beans spiced up with some canned tomato's and green chili's. It was not Moms home cooked meal but it would do. As a surprise, I pulled from my pack, luckily unbroken, a fine bottle of red wine. There wasn't that much yet would allow a glass each. I even felt domestic enough to set the table to look welcoming, all the while envisioning Dove of Spring in her buckskin dress and long black hair.

It was only just past four o'clock so I knew I had a little time to wait before the guys returned. I grabbed some coffee and relaxed and let myself get caught up in the noiseless noise that I so dearly loved.

~ ~ ~ ~

"Boy, talk about disappearing. Where have you been all day ? You didn't even came back for lunch." Mario quizzed.

"Sorry."I answered. "I got caught up in memories and familiarizing myself with the place, I forgot about everything else."

"So what did you discover for us today." Asked Mateo smiling.

"Actually nothing, wise guy. I thought I would leave that up to you for a change."

"I knew it." interrupted Mario with a laugh.

Laughing along with the others I continued.

"But I would like to look at the aerial photo's again.

Particularly the area of the golden treasure."

"Why there ?" inquired Carlos in a more serious tone.

"Just a hunch." I responded. "If you remember the king referenced the western stairway. We never did search it's location. Working with Lone Buffalo back in the desert, he put me on to some reading and legends of tunnel systems through out the south west and some of the readings mentioned the same possible findings in South America."

"That part sort of slipped my mind, but now that you brought it up, yes there are many stories of such tunnels." joined Carlos.

Now my curiosity was really alert.

"I would love to hear some of those stories to see if they tie in with what Dan had remembered."

Diego jumped in with some needed common sense.

"Look guys, we are all interested in this new turn of events but we would have a better attention span on full stomachs."

He was answered with warm smiles and affirmative nods.

"Not a problem." I stated. "I was back a little early and took the liberty of throwing together a few things I found. Supper is ready and waiting. It may not seem like much but until I become familiar with what you do have in the way of supplies, it should do for tonight."

Smiles of thanks and appreciation showed and all joined together at the already prepared table.

"Eat first and talk later." Diego instructed as he poured the wine.

Dinner was a leisurely event with polite discussions, mostly of what they hoped to accomplish in this seasons study. Eric spoke more of his findings at the pyramid site in the desert along with the lost box of contracts from the world wide trade contacts. They all agreed it would take a long time before the established academic community would accept such a thing no matter how real the evidence is. The decipherment of the kings scrolls would also contribute to the validity of both sites. At least so far the Mexican authorities and antiquities people have been most cooperative. They have accepted everything to date. So much of it ties into already known finds and knowledge of the Mayan history. All peoples early history for that matter. A pattern has developed and is always being expanded.

My photographic expertise has proved invaluable and the teams hopes are that I continued to be such an asset. I felt good about my meager contribution hoping even more to shed further light on the past I was intrigued by what my Maya friends had already brought to light and shared my Navajo experiences with them.

Later that evening Diego inquired curiously about Dove of Spring. Lone Buffalo had mentioned to him about the possible romance between the two. Not at all upset by the inquiry I admitted a strong attachment to Violet, but also explained the stronger urge to be where I was today.

"Not unlike any of you." I posed.

The smiles caused by my statement, further proved the truth of everyone's present status.

"Welcome to the stupid bachelors scientific club." commented Mateo. "I guess we all have similar stories." he finished with a smile.

Cleanup went easily and each parted for their hammock. I dwelled on Dove of Spring and her buckskin outfits for quite a while picturing her raven black hair catching all the nuances of light that nature provided. I finally drifted to a peaceful sleep seeing Violet's smile as part of the symphonic orchestrations of the jungle.

Chapter   3

No stranger to the howling monkeys, I awoke with a smile. "Hello my friends," I whispered still smiling.

Heading for the coffee pot I was already thinking of what I would do today. I decided I would leave that up to the other men. After all this was really their project. I stood staring at the tomb of the king remembering the first meeting. The strong smell of the brewing coffee pulled me away from my nostalgia. I poured a mug of the black syrupy liquid and sat down at the table wondering if the team remembered to bring the aerial photographs and stereo glasses.

"I think it would be fun to do some more searching."

I glanced over at the large map of the entire complex that now covered about a mile or two in all directions from the kings tomb. If a major excavation was to be done, I estimated many years of work, and that would be just to get rid of the jungles strangle hold on the structures.

Carlos broke my concentration.

"It's good to be back here isn't it." he said

"It sure is." I answered. "As much as I enjoyed the excitement of discovery in the desert this makes me feel at home. The Maya connection with the Navajo was certainly a plus which is why I stayed so long. They even made me an honorary tribal member for what they said was my contribution."

"Knowing you, I'm sure it was justified also. Look at what you gave us. As far as I'm concerned you are Maya." complimented Carlos.

"I second that." Mario said from behind. "Besides we need you to make coffee."

Within minutes Mateo and Diego joined at the coffee pot.

Once all were comfortably seated I asked about the scroll translations.

Mateo chose to answer. "It's very slow going, but I think eventually we will make a breakthrough. We felt they were much too valuable to bring back to this jungle. They are in safe hands at the college. We have a few chosen students continuing to work on a few of them. The rest are securely locked up. Your photo copies are proving to be most valuable because it preserves the originals."

Pleased at hearing this Eric replied with.,

"Remember you guys, I want to be kept in the loop as to any progress being made. Not only me but the Navajo also want to be kept informed. They in turn will forward any progress they make with the scrolls and contracts they are now studying. This could be a real breakthrough on the history of all peoples."

"Spoken like a true scientist." smiled Carlos.

Eric slightly embarrassed and changing the subject continued.

"Now moving on to today, I wish not to interfere with what ever you have planned. I can assist where possible any one or all of you for that matter. Or if you would like I can free lance on what ever I deem important. However, I would like to view the aerial photo's, that is if you brought them."

"That's where you are in luck my friend, we did bring them. Of course we don't know what we're looking at, but now that you're here hopefully they can be put to good use."

Eric was all smiles now.

"That can be my meager contribution to your study." I replied. "So the decision is now yours." He paused for a few seconds. "What would you have me do ?"

All four scientists smiled. Carlos spoke for all.

"We have many days left to this season. There will be time for you to assist us all. I suggest for now you do what is your specialty. Look at your air photos. Perhaps you can find something new and unique. The city is yours."

He quickly corrected himself smiling. "At least for now. As you well know it belongs to our people of the past. It belongs to history."

All agreed and worked together to fix a healthy breakfast.

I insisted on cleanup after the meal allowing the others to start their day. It wasn't long before I was alone listening to the noise of quiet. Mateo had found the air photo's and set them on the map table along with the stereo viewing glasses.

I sat there at the map table staring at nothing for some ten minutes thinking of all the rumors of hidden tunnel systems throughout both Central and South America. I even recalled the stories of similar legends in North America from New Mexico and Arizona then right up through the Canadian Rockies. But for now I was at home in the Yucatan and that should be my focus. Where to start was the problem. Underground tunnels weren't exactly going to show themselves in aerial pictures saying *"Look, here I am."* I laughed at myself. I felt lost as I refilled my coffee.

My mind blank, with coffee in hand I started walking to the kings tomb.

"No wait stupid, there is nothing there for you regarding this quandary." I said out loud.

I stood there, halfway to the tomb my thoughts searching the file cabinets of my mind.

"The hidden treasure room" That could possibly be a start. If they were trying to hide their treasure from the Spaniards, perhaps there were tunnels to that storage place."

Dumping my coffee I returned to the map table. Sorting the photo's I found both high and low altitude coverage of this particular area. Feeling comfortable and at home again I spread out the needed pictures of the area surrounding the treasure pyramid along with the complimentary topographic maps. Using the pyramid as a focal point I stared my search of the area in all directions referring to the topo-contour map first. This of course would give me an idea of the terrain changes which would possibly hint at hidden mountain ranges, ranges that are so well hidden by the jungle canopy. Some contour changes running southwest of the treasure pyramid triggered something in my overactive mind. It could be my imagination, nevertheless it was worth checking out. I again remembered the king's addressing of the western staircase.

I refilled my coffee a third time as I sorted through the stack of photo's to find the appropriate run. The soft background sounds appeared to fit perfectly with my mood further enhancing my enthusiasm to seriously search along with the simple enjoyment of being here. Finally the correct photo's showed themselves and once laid together I put my eyes to work.

Using the longitude and latitude readings from my "GPS" I pinpointed the exact location of the treasure pyramid. I then transferred that location to the aerial photo's. Unaware of the time, it seemed I spent over two hours back and forth between my three sources; the topo map, and both high and low altitude air photo's.

Sitting back to rest my eyes I then spotted something in the low altitude run. On the northeast side of the pyramid there seemed to be a faint anomaly. *"This certainly wasn't west."* I puzzled. Now that I had a starting point, at least my imagination thought so, I started various arbitrary lines out from the pyramid itself. Establishing a few positive points I felt I had a pattern, or wishful thinking. I immediately moved to the high altitude photo run transferring my wishful thinking points. Sure enough I could detect a continuos line. Not an exact straight lime, but then again mountain ranges are not exactly straight either.

"Enough for now." I told myself.

I needed to take my eyes away from the strain. Getting up I dampened a cloth with some water and softly bathed my eyes. It actually felt refreshing. I rested for a while gazing at distant objects just for the exercise. I could not push past twenty minutes. My excitement would not allow it.

Back to the map table I hurried and reached for the stereo glasses. Starting again at the pyramid site I now studied my made up line in three dimensional viewing fine tuning my line as I went ever so lightly marking pencil dots on the photo's. I continued this 3-D study for about thirty minutes.

Sitting back to view my progress, it appeared I had covered some two and a quarter miles of jungle. After resting for a few minutes I proceeded to transfer my pencil point dots to the low altitude photography. When that was accomplished I transferred the marked locations to a piece of wax paper I borrowed from the kitchen supply tent. I needed a clear overlay for future use and study. I then transposed the same dots from the higher altitude photo run. I now had my two clear, or somewhat clear overlays.

Lost deeply in his thoughts, Eric did not hear Mario approach and was somewhat startled when he heard his voice.

"So now you're playing design engineer, aren't you going

to do any work ?"

I turned quickly to see Mario's huge smile.

"Creating paper work is a very important part of my job. No one understands it so I keep my job secure." I answered with an equal grin.

Eric followed with, "What are you doing here ?"

"My stomach told me it was lunchtime."

"Is it really? " I answered, I had no idea."

As they headed for the kitchen tent the other three wandered in from three different directions.

"How do you guys do it ? I didn't hear any lunch bell." I joked.

As was their habit they all worked together to prepare lunch. Once seated with their meal I conversationally asked.

"Just what is it each of you guys is working on right now ?"

Carlos took the lead to answer.

"Right now what we are doing is rather boring but nevertheless necessary. It's basically nothing more than paper work. The fun of discovery was great for the last two seasons but now the paper recordings must be attended to and in extreme detail along with photo's and hand drawings. As you know it takes years and many people to properly excavate a site and without the proper step by step recordings of what we are doing, actual history could be lost."

Mario filled in from there.

"Chances are we four or five will not be at this site forever. The more thorough we are now the better it will be for those that follow."

That thought had not entered my mind. I felt a twinge of sadness.

"I guess that makes sense. That's pretty much the same path the Navajo are following. A nice advantage that they have is that they are at the same time teaching the younger generation the ways and methods of discovery and recording their research so it stays in the family so to speak. They never move."

Diego interrupted with.

"That's right. Lone Buffalo and I discussed that very thing many times. They live and rule their own land, even though it is a reservation. Their discoveries are their own history."

"They still get a lot of push back from the out side academic community. Their history is sometimes questioned or even doubted by "The Group Who Knows Better." I returned.

"We do get rather cynical at times, don't we." remarked Mateo with a smile.

I smiled in answer, subconsciously agreeing with him.

"I read what ever I can, when ever I can. I don't always agree with what I read, buts that's my choice. I consider myself a free thinker and I like to think outside the box. I believe it gives me a better chance of discovery. Sometimes I'm wrong. I accept that as a learning experience, but at least I do think out side the box and I'm not afraid to do it."

"Whoa there..." Mario said with his hands up. "You don't have to convince us. We're on your side, remember? "

Now flushed with embarrassment I apologized.

"I'm sorry my friends but the rules of the establishment tend to stir me up."

Eric then quickly related the story of Professor Tallman.

"In the meantime." Carlos said "What have you been up to. You're still in the same position as when we left this morning. It must have been a good nap." he added with a smile.

I laughed along with the guys and excitedly told them of my hunch and the studies I had been doing all morning.

"And ?" inquired Mario. "Don't keep us in the dark."

"Actually, nothing yet, I still have some interpretation to do. Let's just say I have a good feeling."

"We like your good feelings." Diego said. "They make us look good. Look what it did for the Navajo."

Diego then went on with a brief outline for Carlos and Mateo of what and how he made a valuable contribution to the tribal history.

The group brain stormed a while longer about Eric's hunch then each went their own way to continue their necessary paperwork. Eric instantly returned to his Aerial Photo's. He re-reviewed, in stereo, his first dot marker on the low altitude photo's. It's position was approximately one hundred and fifty yards from the pyramid in question. Eric studied this for quite sometime. Nothing specific stood out, yet he felt a draw to that spot.

Deciding his eyes had had enough he equipped himself with his camera, a canteen and a machete and started in the direction of the first dot he marked on the photo. After only twenty feet or so he returned to his sleeping area and retrieved his GPS

Gut feel alone told him he was in the right area of approximately one hundred and fifty yards and confirmed by the GPS. It was pure jungle but there were definite terrain changes. The further from the temple the higher the incline went. It was a slow rise but a definite rise. The slight angle of incline made it extremely difficult to detect in the jungle overgrowth showing on the photo run. Eric, by now had his adrenalin running full speed.

Retracing his path back to the temple he decided to employ the techniques Carlos had showed him by studying the vegetation for its well hidden human interference. It also then dawned on him that there might not be an exit/entrance to a mountain tunnel. That would mean a walk, even though a short distance, to the temple carrying their golden treasures. That would make them subject to discovery. Eric's thoughts went to the desert pyramid. That treasure room was totally below ground level. Who knows, perhaps there was yet an undiscovered tunnel entrance. He would have to have Lone Buffalo follow up on that in the desert pyramid as he would do himself here.

Deciding to end his search for the day he returned to camp. His thoughts were to ask the crew to humor him so all could participate in a search for hidden entrance ways into the mountains.

When they were all comfortable around the dinner table I made my pitch. I prefaced the whole thing with a detailed replay of my day. Knowing of my luck in the past their interest was there. Mateo brought up the fact he thought they had done a pretty thorough look when it was first discovered. I did not disagree with him but went on to emphasize how Dan and I accidently found doors and panels that led to more discoveries. I felt it was worth another try. There were always the words of the king of a western stairwell.

They toasted with their water cups to give it a shot tomorrow. If nothing else it would be a break from the boredom of paper work.

Chapter 4

It was a lazy morning, a long leisurely breakfast but each of the five could feel the excitement building. Just after nine they geared up with flashlights, machete's and camera equipment and off they went to the tomb.

I also mentioned the other site Carlos and I had come across, shaped like a parallelogram , walled in by trees both planted and cut, the major part of which was underground. I knew we wouldn't get to it today but hoped the other guys would be willing to go, perhaps tomorrow, or another day soon. None of us had thoroughly investigated that site as of yet, even though there was some preliminary work done with Frank two years ago. I finally gave up for lack of interest , at this time anyway.

The rest of the day was taken up with the five of us double and triple checking every floor, wall and ceiling of the whole tomb structure.

The mood was quite jovial with me being the object of never ending jokes and jabs at my lucky streak having run out.

That same light and airy mood enabled time to fly. By four o'clock that afternoon we had thoroughly searched all that was possible and headed back to base camp. Having ignored lunch, our appetites were ravenous. Naturally we all pitched in on dinner preparations.

As hard as the hands and knees work was, the day was most enjoyable and time passed quickly. Totally at ease after such a relaxed day we all lit up cigars and just veged out. I decided this was the perfect time to ply my bribery surprise. Deep in my pack I had secreted a bottle of Remy Martin Cognac. They eagerly accepted my token of thanks. Having successfully delivered my bribe I then asked in my most humble way about the underground temple. I explained how it made sense to me that since it was purposely made to be underground, it would stand to reason that there had to be an entrance somewhere and that entrance could be the termination of a tunnel. As an added incentive I reiterated the story of the tunnel in the sandstone mountain in the desert.

They collectively picked up on that and asked rhetorically why a tunnel at all in the mountain. That now became the evenings discussion. They had all heard of tales of hidden tunnels throughout South America. They were not exactly convinced these stories were factual.

I begged nicely for their help for just one day. I knew they would really not refuse but they did give me a difficult time for close to a half hour, all the while laughing and smiling.

Since I had not really researched the air photo's of that area we came to a happy compromise. They would go back to their boring paperwork while I spent the day playing interpreter again, and on the next day the five of us would head for the temple and underground room of gold. They all finally agreed to my compromise solution since there was no cognac left.

The balance of the night was fun as always. The change of jungle music from daytime orchestrations to night time symphonies signaled bed time which none of us ignored.

"Good night Violet and thank you, I hope all is well."

My special music closed my eyes for the night.

Chapter 5

My four Mayan friends left just after breakfast leaving me to my photo searching. It was still tugging at my brain about not finding another hidden door in the treasure room. To me, living in today's world it just didn't make sense to have that many valuables stored in one place. How did they get it all there with out the Spaniards knowledge. I'll have to question the guys about that again. I was also disappointed about the anomalies I found, or should I say didn't find, in the aerial photo's just outside the pyramid.

Oh well, back to the drawing board as they say. It took me a while to find the photo's of the area in question. Then I remembered it was my own fault. I was so anxious the other day to locate the coverage by the tomb that I did not pay attention to how or where I was putting the pictures I discarded at the time. Now I was paying the price.

It was almost ten o'clock by the time I got myself straightened out. I grabbed another mug of coffee and set my eyes to work. "This complex appears very different looking at it this way."I mumbled to myself aloud."

Carlos was sure that the larger part of the structure was built underground. This is even bigger than I imagined when we scoped it out on the ground." I switched my focus from the temple site to the surrounding area, all directions. Just northwest of the temple I noticed something that did not fit with the surrounding environs. The tree pattern did not appear to match. Shuffling again through the now better organized photo's I located the lower altitude photo run. Sure enough, the same mis matched pattern. The trees, though just as thick, seemed to be of a lesser height the closer they were to the temple area. This fits in with what Carlos had pointed out to me on our original discovery. I resumed my eye search totally around the site stretching out at least five hundred feet in all directions. There was nothing else that caught my eye that looked anything like the anomaly I found on the northwest side. Checking the Topo map it all fit in. There was a small range of mountains or at least higher terrain, that ran in a northeast southwest direction across the area. I marked the photo and the map of my point of interest. Tomorrow we would have a better idea. I plugged the coordinates into the GPS as a starting point for tomorrow.'

        Still bothered by not finding anything yesterday I resolved on one more look at the photos. I grabbed another mug of coffee while resting my eyes staring curiously at the pyramid tomb.

"You are on the right path my friend. Do not let your frustration defeat you."

        I was wondering if the king was going to help me. Of course he didn't tell me anything but now I know not to quit. I did not try to answer his words of encouragement already knowing it would have been futile. I just sat down at the map table when one by one my friends returned for lunch. I still marveled how they all arrived basically at the same time.

        It was a quick lunch with out much conversation and again one by one they disappeared into the jungle in different directions.

        Concentrating on the photo's in stereo viewing I flipped back and forth between the high and low pictures. Nothing more became apparent than what I originally picked up on. Not heeding the kings words I could feel myself getting frustrated. I finally determined it was my own over confidence. I was spoiled by my previous success.

        It was time for physical searching again. I picked up my three necessary tools; camera, GPS and machete and hurried into the dark green canopy. I think I pretty well judged where the treasure room was and proceeded with my search. As I moved closer to the pyramid, Carlos's quick lesson in jungle greenery took hold. I did see some minor differences. Because of the color, as he pointed out, it suddenly became obvious that some of the vegetation was obviously younger. It was up to me to decide now whether it was only younger because it was an area cleared for the allowance to build the pyramid or was it replanted to hide a secret entrance. I started to mark a line where I thought one ended and the other began. I did this by breaking branches. When all was said and done I had an area roughly twenty feet wide running parallel to the west side of the tomb. This pleased me, yet I warned myself about getting over confident. I broadened my search area, both wider and deeper into the surrounding jungle. A few areas of new -vs- old growth did show up but were nondescript areas covering two or three feet. The actual jungle growth did not look disturbed.

My stomach reminded me of lunch but I was too worked up to leave now. I returned to my original find and started a more detailed study. If I stood with my back to the west side of the pyramid and viewed straight out, a slight incline in the terrain could be imagined. To me that was a good enough start. I made up my mind to track that way for a distance to see if my suspicion was correct. I walked and slashed for about forty minutes. The view behind me was not the clearest because of the jungle growth but it was for certain I had traveled at an up incline. Resting for a few minutes I seemed to be regaining some faith in myself. Even if it proves to be nothing, at least I know my eyes were not deceiving me in what I saw on the photo. I started my return to the Temple at a very slow pace. Trying not to let any detail skip my view. I checked every tree base, every crevice, every rock and even every leaf I thought looked different.

Out of pure frustration I heard myself saying.

"Atl, please help me."

Of course I did not expect to get an answer. I suddenly felt a strange tingle. The jungle itself became still.

"As usual, Eric, you are doing well without my help. The path you have chosen will satisfy your curiosity. Forsake not your quest."

Knowing I was alone again I muttered aloud.

"Why does he do this to me. I am not a chosen one, nor will I ever be. Perhaps I should have stayed in the desert. Dove of Spring accepted me for who I was. She made no attempt to change me.

Eric let out a loud gasp of exasperation. Along with that the jungle sounds returned. He laughed at himself as he took a drink from his canteen.

"I actually feel better now. Okay, "Chosen One" back to work."

I laughed with and at myself.

"That's funny." I thought to myself. *"That's the first time I spoke of Violet in such a positive way. Maybe I am changing."*

I was now back at my starting point, the first dot I marked on the photo. I sat and rested again to build up my strength for the hands and knees searching I was about to embark on. I let the jungle music sooth me while I just sat there staring at the edge of what looked like a square cut rock. Actually there were two of them. Not in any particular order either. Just lying askew half hidden by the thick undergrowth. I continued to enjoy my daytime serenade when it suddenly hit me.

"Square cut rocks. ? What are square cut rocks doing this far away from the pyramid ?"

I scrambled to my feet, which really did not work too well because I moved too fast with out thinking and found myself face down in prickly under growth.

"Oh well, what's a little blood among friends."

I again struggled to my feet and moved slowly to the rocks in question. They had obviously been in place for quite some time. On close and careful inspection of the surrounding area I discovered three more, smaller in size and almost overgrown by the reclamation of nature. I took a few pictures first then started in with my machete. My goal was to clear enough ground to determine if there were any man made ground disturbances. My mind started to grow doubts as I hacked away.

"Why build an entrance this far away from the pyramid. If this was truly a tunnel, why not go directly into the tomb itself. I continued slashing even as my doubts grew. Totally sweat soaked I was about to quit to rest, when my machete struck something solid, which of course sent a vibrating pain cruising up my arm. I dropped the machete screaming a few expletives I don't normally use. Once the vibrations stopped the pain dissipated. It was then I realized I hit another cut block. My arm sort of back to normal I renewed my clearing efforts. I convinced myself that something man made was definitely here. There were many blocks scattered through out a ten foot area. Some large, most smaller in size. Small enough to be carried by one man. Totally exhausted and quite hungry, common sense told me to quit for the day and I knew it was getting late. I cheered myself up knowing I would have promised assistance tomorrow. After a short rest I slowly walked back to camp.

I must have really looked bedraggled because when I was spotted by my friends I could see the concern on the faces. Choosing to speak first to belay their fears I said with a smile,

"Hi guys. I feel much better than I probably look. I have a lot to tell you."

I knew that would pique their interest, which it did. However, their genuine concern for my well being made me feel even better.

Lucky for me they had supper ready. I did not have to be asked twice to partake. I wolfed down everything they gave me not even caring what it was. I mumbled with my mouth full that I would tell all after I ate. They laughed as they watched me pig out, making all kinds of snide remarks.

"It's great to have good friends." I thought.

My appetite sated I sat back and sincerely thanked them for my dinner. I could tell by their eyes they were more than anxious to hear of my day. I related the whole story dragging out the suspense. As expected they were all aglow when I came to the end. I told them exactly where I left off, nothing concrete but promising. I could feel them gauging my words and that I wasn't pulling their legs.

"I'm going back there in the morning to pick up where I left off." I said happily. I want to follow this through."

Diego was the first to speak.

"It would go faster if two of us were digging."

"Or three." said Mario

"Or four." joined Mateo.

"I don't want to be left alone, so let's make it five." Carlos said. "But." he appended. "You owe us another bottle of cognac.

Feeling a little overcome with their willingness, I smiled and promised each their own bottle of cognac. Of course we joked about that for a while until I politely excused myself and went to my hammock. I was exhausted. I said good night to Dove of Spring and tuned into my favorite melody.

Chapter 6

Breakfast was over and done with early with all five anxious to see what possible discovery lay ahead. Besides their usual machete as their major tool they each brought along a military type entrenching tool, a folding shovel and pick ax combination which folded for easy carrying.

Eric did not have to say when they arrived at the place of interest. It was now that obvious thanks to his digging and clearing yesterday.

My friends were right away interested in the square cut blocks that were scattered about. Carlos even took the time to go back to the tomb pyramid to check a theory he had. He was convinced he was right. These small blocks were taken from the main tomb to use. There has to be a reason for that. He speculated but would not make a commitment until he further investigated his theory.

We all worked feverishly for close to two hours and it was still just after ten In the morning. Of course there was always the joking back and forth, most of which was aimed at me.

Out of the blue Mateo yelled for our attention.

"Guys, Guys, I found something. At least I think I have."

We all rushed to his area. Sure enough there were many felled trees in one region, that when you think of it, appear out of place. The logs were in disarray but it was organized chaos, if there is such a thing.

Carlos, the one most familiar with structures of the past studied the tract in question. After a few minutes of silent walking around the downed trees he finally spoke in a serious professional tone,

"It wouldn't be the first time they meant to deceive others.

Chances are there is something here. Perhaps a hidden entrance or even a hidden tunnel."

He looked directly at me when he said this

"What I was thinking of though is not the obvious. In other words, what ever we may be searching for, my guess is that it is not at the center of this jungle debris, but also not far away."

"All is not what it appears to be. Your friend is on the right path Eric. Travel not far, but in the direction of your desires."

Of course, as soon as I wanted to question Atl further he was gone. I looked to Mario and Diego. They showed no sign of having heard the king. I decided then not to mention this most recent mental message. I added my two cents to what Carlos just imparted, talking about keeping the alignment with the western exposure of the pyramid. Carlos agreed with my thinking. Carlos, then sort of took charge.

"Okay guys, let's fan out from the center of the log pile and start."

"Start what ?" Mateo asked confused.

"Looking, digging, chopping, stomping, I don't care. Just start searching. I don't even know what for. We'll know when we find it."

"This reminds me of Dan and I tapping with the rebar till we heard something different."

Moving through the underbrush something caught my eye. There was a spot about three feet square that had only low growing vegetation. The normal underbrush was between three and five feet tall, with thick stalks. This one spot looked like low growing weeds by comparison. I stopped for a more thorough scrutiny. Using my machete like I did the rebar in the desert, I started probing straight down. It was so much easier in the desert. This ground was unforgiving and packed like cement under the torrential rains and heat of the jungle. With some extra effort I finally did break through the surface. Two to three inches down the dirt gave way and I was able to get the full length of the machete buried. I pulled it out and roughly gauged the length to be three feet. Moving some distance over I tried again with the same beginning effort, again it went to the hilt. I tried a third time after moving yet again. The blade only went about two feet in before hitting something solid. I automatically figured it was a rock. I moved again pushed at my machete rebar. Just over two feet I heard a thud.

"Same rock ?" I wondered. I tried moving in another direction. The thud noise reappeared. Excitedly I called.

"Hey guys, Over here ! We may have something !" I called with half smiles and I told you so in my eyes.

They gathered around waiting for my explanation. Rather than try to explain I figured I would just demonstrate. I jammed the big knife into the ground and with some effort it went up to the hilt. I looked to the group who were silently staring at me questioning. I smiled and said

"Just wait."

Moving to one of my earlier spots I repeated the knife stab. After only about two feet we all heard the thud. My friends were now smiling with me as all started jabbing the ground. Twenty minutes passed and we now had a roughly four by four foot outline. I looked at the group again

"Now we start digging."

With that they all turned away and started back to camp.

"Where are you going." I yelled.

Mario stopped, turned to look at me saying.

"This morning you said we would help you look. We did that. You said nothing about digging."

"Okay, okay ! I'll fix dinner tonight."

Laughing now they returned and started digging.

"Since when did you guys join an organized union." I asked. Of course I received no answer. *They must be taking lessons from the king.* I thought.

With all of us putting forth a decent effort into this mission of hopeful discovery, it wasn't too long when we were gawking at a wooden platform about four foot square. There was no logical reason this should be here except to hide something. At least so we thought.

"Oh for a backhoe right now." I mumbled.

This, of course brought some light laughter.

"You just got spoiled by digging in the soft desert sand."

Mario quipped."

"You're probably right." I replied while starting to dig at the edge of the log platform. Soon everyone was digging and scratching at the four by four outline. Mateo was the first to break through to a hollow. Excitement filled the air. Diego and I moved to that spot to help make a larger hole. We didn't get too deep though. It was filled with rocks both big and small. WE tried digging under the platform. There was nothing but rock and jungle debris dried and rotten now of course. We trained our digging on all four sides of the wooden area only to find the same thing.

In the meantime Carlos and Mario moved about four feet away and started digging. Once having dug through the top foot and a half the ground was easier to manipulate. Down they went. Mateo and I spelled them when they tired out. I gauged we were down about eight feet when Carlos called for a halt. We gave no argument. You could see he was thinking.

"Before we get too carried away and wear ourselves out for nothing. Start digging sideways to the platform."

Diego and Mario took over for us and started probing ninety degrees to the hole we were in. They had not gone more than two and a half feet when they came upon rock and debris.

"Hold up for now." Carlos suggested. "If my thinking is right, we will get no where if we continue to pursue this. We all sent questions with our eyes while he slowly resumed his thinking out loud.

"Something is definitely down here, but the hole was purposely back filled to help keep others out. The question is how deep ?" Carlos stated and surveyed the distance to the tomb. "It's not just the distance but more importantly the depth. In general what do you think the height difference is between here and the treasure room ?"

It dawned on the rest of us then. There had to be a significant difference. Remember the treasure room was at least thirty feet below ground level at the pyramid site and where we were presently was probably at least fifty plus feet above the tombs ground level."

Mario voiced what the rest of us were thinking.

"So we could be looking at roughly eighty plus or minus feet of rocks and rubble. Which of course with out modern equipment and machinery would tale us weeks to dig out."

I quickly interrupted.

"So this really could be a tunnel and at one time may have connected with the treasure room. Once the treasure was safely hidden away, this and possibly more areas were forever closed.'

"Exactly." Carlos replied.

I immediately interrupted again thinking aloud.

"So I was possibly correct in thinking of another hidden door in the treasure room."

"But we looked and found nothing." Mateo joined.

"Yes, but that doesn't mean there isn't a hidden panel some place. I for one am going to look again. You guys can join me if you want but I just have to follow this up."

"Can we rest a bit first." asked Diego. "I'm tired."

A long rest was unanimous.

Leaving the digging as it was we headed back to the camp and lunch.

"I know you will all think I'm crazy but my patience is running out. That small snack I had will hold me till supper. I just have to get to the treasure room."

"Okay." chided Mario. "We'll finish lunch, that will give you time to find the door to the tunnel. We'll meet you there and walk the tunnel with you."

I started walking but turned around and like a child stuck my tongue out at them while my thumb was at my nose waving the other four fingers.

In a way I was glad I was alone. Perhaps I can attain the help of Atal. I took a long hard look at the treasure room again realizing, based on what Atal said, the tunnel entrance could not be in this room. I went to the circular hallway that surrounded the treasure room with its many portals. I wondered if the compass will work this far underground. I proceeded to walk the curved passageway watching the compass needle. It had a mind of its own and pointed every which way. I closed it up and returned it to my pocket. I now felt totally disorientated. How do I determine which way is west. I stood there for a few minutes in the middle of the circular corridor housing the treasure room. My compass was useless because of the magnetic variations of the underground ores and minerals.

I was again delighted that I was alone so that no one could see what I was about to do.

I first returned to the outer part of the pyramid and positively determined a western heading. Without seriously moving my body from that position I reentered the tomb, and navigated my way back to the circular hallway by keeping my body in one position. I ended up walking backwards, sideways both right and left until I reached a portion of the circle where I was facing the wall head on. I must have looked a sight. It was also challenging trying to negotiate the stairway. Thank goodness for the automatic lighting. Oh well, no matter how it happened I felt confident I was now facing the western wall. Disappointingly, a very blank wall. Just to be on the safe side I scratched an X where I was standing with my pocket knife. That I decided was the easy part. I now faced a blank wall. A quick cursory examination showed me nothing. No lines, cracks, scratches, indents, bumps, nothing. But there has to be something. Atal spoke of a western stairwell. This is west to the best of my knowledge, so where's the steps.

Eric feeling himself getting impatient and frustrated took a deep breath and looked around for Mr. Blue, then laughed at himself,

"Maybe I am losing it." he said aloud.

"Not totally my friend, not yet anyway."

I spun around to see Carlos and Diego. Before I could find my voice Carlos resumed,

"Obviously you figured out which way is west. So now what ?"

"I don't really know." I answered a little self conscious.

"If I may Eric, I have been doing a lot of thinking about these ancient structures. Our ancestors were masters of hiding things. I think you're on the right track just in the wrong place."

Now even I was confused and apparently it showed on my face. With a warming smile Carlos continued." If you recall there are two portals, one on either side of where you are standing. Both seem to go no where, both are in the general direction of west. There is where I suggest we try looking."

I hesitated for a while taking in what Carlos just outlined.

The light of recognition finally went on in my head. Suddenly talking out loud to no one in particular.

"I should have realized that. Every thing to date has always been a puzzle, why should this be any different.." Gazing directly at Carlos I commented, "Thank you my friend. Sometimes I believe I confuse myself because I become too excited with the unknown."

Carlos laughed along with me and we started for the portal to our left.

"I'll check out the one on the right." Diego shared.

Just then Mario showed and joined Diego.

The anticipation of a possible new discovery was making my heart race a little. I quickly peeked at Carlos hoping it wasn't obvious. Through the portal about ten feet we started checking the usual bumps, cracks and edges, etc. hoping for a hidden latch of sorts. Nothing showed itself but that did not mean there was nothing. Just as Carlos and I stared at each other we heard Diego's all too distinct voice.

"Come quick ! I think I found something !"

He and Mario were about fifteen feet inside the portal both with grins. The smile was contagious, so we joined in not knowing why.

"You're the expert Carlos, take a look at this." Diego said.

He pointed to a seam that ran from floor to ceiling. It was barely visible but it was definitely a straight seam. Turning instantly serious Carlos inquired.

"Just the one ?"

Not waiting for an answer he followed with,

"Keep looking, see if you can find another one."

Turning to the wall itself he put his talented fingers to work. Having exercised his technique many times myself I joined him at the wall. The area was eerily silent except for the sound of the fingers gently sanding the surface. Again the hush was disturbed by Diego.

"I don't see any other seams."

"Except." joined Mario.

"There appears to be a dark line or seam here at the corner."

Carlos stepped away from the wall gauging the distance. He guessed it to be approximately ten feet. He then started looking at the floor and identifying some scuff marks he softly exclaimed.

"A center pivot wall."

Smiles could be seen on all our faces.

Carlos continued as if talking to himself.

"This looks about right for the middle. I'll need something to stand on in order to reach the top."

Without being asked Mario and Diego turned and left the area. Five minutes later they returned carrying two large boxes. Carlos did nothing more than nod his head as he stacked the boxes where he wanted them. With his arm outstretched and standing on tip toe his trained fingers were working their magic. An almost imperceptible click was heard followed by a low rumble of stone as the wall began to pivot open just about where Carlos was standing. The movement was very slow with a few grumbling hesitations. The stale air and gas fumes starting to escape signaled us all to move and move quickly.

Once safely outside we were joined by Mateo.

"Looks like I missed all the fun." he said straight faced. Then added with a half smile. "I see you remembered about the poison gas the king mentioned." holding up five bandana's. Each of us hurriedly grabbed one.

It was agreed we should wait at least forty five minutes to be on the safe side. We were all expressing our opinions as to what we would find. It wasn't treasure we were talking about either. The thought of the legends of long lost tunnels coming to fruition was almost too much to bare.

Carlos, the one who was always the most logical, was even showing signs of excitement.

The forty five minutes seemed like an eternity even though we understood the necessity for it. I read about forty seven minutes had passed.

"Shall we give it a try ?"

We all rose to our feet from our lazy positions and started for the tomb passage way.

"Wait !" cried Carlos, "I think it would be prudent that only one of us go and check out the air. When it is considered safe we can all go in."

Bowing to his common sense I volunteered to go. I received no challenge. Affixing the wet bandana over my nose and mouth

I willingly entered the pyramid. I tested the air periodically by lifting up and breathing but not too deeply. I got to the pivotal door with high hopes. The air was relatively clear but on looking further my hopes were dashed on the rocks. Literally on the rocks. Piles of broken rock mixed with decayed jungle debris filled the cavern behind the door. I stood there motionless, speechless, wanting to cry. I don't know how long I was frozen there. The hand on my shoulder brought me back to the living. It was Carlos, eventually followed by the others. My disappointment showing heavily I slumped down against the wall across from the opening. Diego, trying to keep the situation light chided with,

"Don't worry Pal, you can't win them all."

I stood up a bit but did not smile. Diego extended his arm and helped me up.

"Chances are ," Carlos said. "These rocks and debris go all the way to our digging up on the hill."

"That may be." I thought. *"But that doesn't exactly fit with what Atal spoke of earlier. He referred to the gasses as if the tunnel was active. I must talk to him as soon as possible."*

"Well, it was a good try Eric. Perhaps we'll find a tunnel system yet, just not here. Okay guys, back to our boring paper work."

As we all started to leave I mentioned, purposely on the loud side,.

"I guess I'll go back to camp and start preparing dinner. Thanks guys."

~ ~ ~ ~

I was glad to be alone again hoping I could contact Atal. He owed me for this. I went straight to my hammock and stretched out. I wasn't tired, I just wanted quiet to concentrate.

"I know you can hear me Atl. Please answer. It is very important."

I lay there in the melodic noise of the jungle. My mind shifted to the peace this place always gave me. Before I knew it Dove of Spring was here. At least in my mind she was. Perhaps my attraction to this woman is stronger than I thought. Going back to her is not such a bad thing. I recalled the words of Whispering Wind.

"She will always be there my friend. Her commitment is true. The decision of the future, your future, is strictly up to you. We often do not see what is before our eyes."

"I'm beginning to believe that now. But for now I am here and I chose, right or wrong, to be here."

"I sense there is something on your mind Eric, Can I be of assistance ?"

"You know damned well what is on my mind. I and my friends have just gone through an extreme amount of work all for naught. I feel you have led me astray."

"How so Eric. Your ability to find things has always been a sense of pride to me. How have I led you astray ? If I did so, it was not my intent."

I calmed myself down somewhat to curb my anger and frustration.

"You spoke of a staircase and poison gasses and the like. We have just spent many hours searching and digging only to find a hole full of rocks and debris. There is no western stairway."

"I have just now observed your work effort. I'm quite sure it was considerably tedious. That which you dug is not the western stairway. It was meant to be an anti chamber to the pyramid. Someone misinterpreted the original plan and started in the wrong location. It was, is, and always will be nothing."

The king was silent then.
"Not now. Don't go away now. You have not helped me."

"Your fears are unwarranted my friend. Exactly

what is it you wish?"

The western stairway. How do I locate it. I am at a total loss at this point."

"That is not like you Eric. Do not lose faith in your own abilities. If I recall my exact words I'll repeat. "I also sense you are looking for an outside entrance, and you are right in doing so. It has not been used in over four hundred years. Beware of its dangers."

"Yes, I remember." I casually remarked.

"Poisonous gasses abound from thermal columns and you must ascend the western staircase."

"Yes, I remember that also."

"You enter the eastern steps. You must leave by the western steps."

"Yes, but where are they." I asked in frustration.

"Think not about portals as you know them. Did you not descend two sets of steps to gain access to the sacred room of gifts ? Did you not realize the deeper steps were of western inclination."

"So what you are saying is that an exterior entrance lies there ?"

"You have always done well without me, my friend. Why should you need me now ?"

I knew by those words I was dismissed. My frustrations clouded my judgement right now. I lay there feeling sorry for myself. Why did Atal always have to talk in riddles. I tried to listen to my jungle serenade to clear my mind..

Riddle, riddle, riddle. My mind surprisingly started to work again. The inevitable light bulb finally lit up.

"**W**hy you big dummy. You walked past it a dozen times," I scolded myself.

I moved so quickly to get out of my hammock I ended up on the ground looking up at it.

"**S**erves you right you idiot. Next time pay attention to what you're doing."

Laughing quietly to myself again I sat there checking for any major bodily damage. Luckily I was okay. Collecting myself I made straight for the tomb.

~ ~ ~ ~ ~

I almost felt light headed. I was so happy to have my head back on straight. I arrived at the second set of steps and recited to myself the kings words.

"You must ascend the western stairs."

Okay, let's pretend I have just come up the stairs. What now.

"**L**ook for an opening Dummy. I chastised myself for the third time.

Using a small pocket flash light I gazed straight ahead. Studying the wall, which at this point was made up of many cut blocks just like the outside structure of the pyramid., made it easy to imagine a doorway of sorts. I moved closer and using my flash light I started a detailed examination of the wall. I consumed the next half hour moving ever so slowly side to side and up and down, blanketing the whole wall, marking certain spots with scratches. Standing back to view my handy work it appeared I had covered a span of seven feet floor to ceiling by fifteen feet side to side. My next step was to visually connect to dots or scratch marks in this case. My final drawing showed a possible shape except it was longer than it was high. It also followed the outline of the varied cut block.

"Why not." I thought.

Carlos said the ancestors were masters of hiding. I chipped a corner from one of the blocks to use like chalk and actually outline and connect the dots. Distant viewing again showed what could be an existing doorway. From the extreme irregular shape, I guessed it to be a center pivot method.

"Listen to me. Now I'm an expert."

Now to find the trigger switch.

I could feel my anxiety building so I purposely took a break. I sat down, and took some deep breaths. I let my thoughts wander to Violet and her farewell kiss. I had enjoyed my mini vacation but brought myself back to the present. Feeling enthused but no longer anxious I set to work looking for the key to unlock the door. Much to my surprise it did not take long. I felt the indent, heard a noise and the wall started moving. It moved as I predicted it would. I waited for the air change protected by my bandana. I gave the air exchange thirty minutes or so before I stepped into the opening. It was a smaller opening than I would have thought. More than wide enough for one man but not quite for two together. The walls were bare and rough, as was the ceiling and floor. I soon became aware of a major problem. There was no lighting. I guess they deemed it unnecessary to put their self powered illumination in this space.

"Exactly what is this space ?" I asked myself.

I couldn't go too far with out a lantern, which of course I did not have with me and I knew my pocket flash light was far from adequate for the task. Which meant I would have to go back to camp. Because of the time and my promise to fix dinner, I called it quits.

I will discuss my find at dinner.

Chapter 7

I barely got set up for dinner when one by one my friends wandered into camp. Eventually we were all settled at the table with our choice of MRE's. I said I would fix dinner, I didn't say it would be fancy.

Every one exchanged stories about their boring day double checking paper work. We all agreed with Frank in one thing. This particular lost city and its treasure trove would be the find of the century. Soon it became my turn to talk about my afternoon. I quietly and without emotion said.

"I found what could be the tunnel entrance. It was getting late and I did not have time to thoroughly investigate. I promised I would take care of dinner, and keeping a promise was more important then following new discoveries.

The excitement of all four was now directed at me.

"Where is it ? How did you find it ? What's there ?"

These questions and more were fired at me by all.

I sat there wearing a slight grin allowing my tease to continue. Totally frustrated they finally gave up, sat back and Mario said "WELL ?"

Having had my fun, I gave in and quietly explained my whole day in extreme detail. By the time we finished with Q & A it was later than expected. A good nights sleep was warranted.

In my hammock, listening to my symphony of the night I said my good night to Dove of Spring. For reasons unknown I concentrated more than usual, sending my warmest thoughts to her, hoping to activate the way of the king and Whispering Wind. I truly wanted to communicate my feelings to her.

The   next thing I knew   the howler monkeys were screeching me awake.

~ ~ ~ ~ ~ ~

The coffee seemed extra special this morning probably because I had such a happy and restful sleep. There was still a hint of Violet on my mind but I must now face the excitement of discovery. At least we all hoped so.

Breakfast hurriedly over we headed for the tomb.

As excited as I was I let the others go first waiting for there reactions. I knew they were at the doorway, even though I was at the tail end of the line, but I didn't hear any exciting remarks. Suddenly the joking started; of course I was the recipient. I made my way to a closed door. The disappointment must have showed on my face, hence all became quiet.

"Honest guys, this was the opening. I don't understand."

"Do you remember what you did to open it ?" inquired Carlos.

"Of course," I answered feeling a slight hurt by his question.

"Then do it again." he said smiling.

I went right to the spot, moving my fingers as I did the day before and Bingo. The stone rumble was heard.

Carlos, talking directly to me finally explained.

"It has been from my experience in readings that these doors are made purposely to close by them selves. This seals the fate of any unwanted intruders. How this takes place I have no idea, nor does anyone else that I know. Who knows ? We may never find out."

"That's good to know, I would hate to get trapped in a vault like this." I answered thankfully.

The five of us stood staring just as I did yesterday. Remembering the high powered lanterns we carried, one by one they were lit. We were viewing an obvious long tunnel. Even from where we stood you could see the slightest incline. Who knows where it leads. As anxious as we were, there was a hesitation about going into the unknown.

"For safety sake." suggested Mateo. "Not all of us sho_ld go at the same time."

Who could disagree with that.

"I'll stay here." I posed. "You guys decides who goes a second group can go at another time."

The others all began to laugh at the same time. Mario moved to me, stood behind me and pushed me to the tunnel.

"Now that's settled."

"Eric, this is your dream, your tunnel., your hard work, so naturally you should go first. We'll draw straws to see who goes with you. The rest of us will await your return and share in your glory."

It was very clear I was outnumbered which also made me very happy. It was my dream.

Mario was chosen to accompany me into the secrets of hundreds of years ago.

We took off slowly, each sporting a lantern. The first hundred feet or so showed nothing except the craftsmanship of carving out the tunnel. Today's subway and tunnel builders would be highly impressed. Mario and I had not said a word aloud but were still happily communicating, thanks to the king.

There was a very slight curve in the tunnel but it continues up hill ever so slowly. Rounding the bend was our first surprise. Two totally uniformed conquistadors lying face down, each with two long arrows in their back. This had been their resting place for over four hundred years.

Mario and I both said a few words for them, being that we were the closest thing to a funeral that they had. Mario speculated that they must have found a way into the tunnel unknown to their fellow soldiers. They were probably missed but never found. The Mayan ancestors were only protecting their culture.

We continued on, curiosity building. We came upon another bend to the left. We figured we were now about two hundred yards away from the pyramid. I suddenly had a crazy idea. I mentioned to Mario that the next curve we come two would be to the right.

"What makes you say that ?" he asked

Than within seconds he answered his own question.

"The rubble pile we were digging up. The tunnel was built

to curve around it." he voiced aloud to a slight echo.

"You're absolutely correct. That had to be it. So now we know where we are corresponding to above ground. But where does the tunnel go from here ?"

"Only one way to find out." was my answer.

On we went, communicating by mind only was working well. We were almost at the point where we were reading each others thoughts aside from the conversing.

The construction of this underground passage was mind boggling. Neither one of us could come up with the how's and without the large earth moving machinery of today. As I said, mind boggling. Periodically we would come across a Glyph scratched into the stone. Totally unfamiliar to us both.

We kept moving on, using only one lantern now, to conserve the battery. We agreed we had come at least one mile with no end in sight. We also agreed to be walking with less effort. In other words we were not ascending any more on a regular basis. A small incline every now and then was all that showed itself. Another fact dawned on me which I shared with Mario instantly.

"The air." I announced. "The air is not stale. The air is reasonably fresh. Being this far and deep underground one would think the air would be stale and lacking oxygen. It's not super fresh, but it is certainly not lacking oxygen."

"You're right. There must be ventilation in this cavern somewhere."

"Just another wonder of engineering to add to the ancestors talents," I praised.

A short distance later I signaled a stop. I asked Mario if he noticed anything different. It took a few seconds of concentration on what I asked when he announced in the affirmative.

"The air," he said quietly. "It appears somewhat clearer here."

Then the Glyph on the wall caught his attention as it caught mine a while ago. It took some additional thinking from both of us to put two and two together.

"Outside air or ventilation," he verbalized.

"And the Glyph's are marking the areas," I added.

"Come to think of it the Glyph's are all alike," Mario added.

"Exactly right, my friend."

We both felt better knowing we had discovered something. We then started searching by the Glyph for some sort of hole or ventilator tube, but to no avail. We decided to leave that for another time as we renewed our exploration of the unknown.

Still only using one lantern they figured they could go on for another hour before having to return. The vent Glyphs continued to appear like clockwork.

Mario then even suggested that an upper entrance could be possible at these vent stations. I could not disagree with him but again that kind of a search would have to wait.

We traveled for that other hour with no new results. We did not absolutely want to yet knew we must start our return trip. More of us could do this tomorrow. Our return walk was as uneventful as our original incursion.

Supper, was of course, filled with excitement and a barrage of questions, which Mario and I answered, each and every one. It was decided Mario and I would stay behind tomorrow while the other three walked the tunnel. Thinking ahead we made sure they took a lunch of sorts.

Down deep inside I wanted to continue my explore but I knew in all fairness the other three should go. I will definitely go the next trip even if I have to go alone.

Chapter 8

Carlos, Diego and Mateo were on their way at a few minutes before eight the next morning. Mario wished to continue his written documentation and did not need my help. I went back to my aerial photo work. Who knows what could turn up. It was a way to pass the time anyway.

Certain feelings led me back to the tunnel theory on the air photos. Without the proper survey tools and compass or GPS headings there was really no way of knowing where the tunnel was running. True there was a way, and relatively accurate also, to map or plot the tunnel but that would take many more hours of concentrated work. In good conscience I could not ask my friends to interrupt their important historical work to follow a whim of mine.

So here I am, happily back with my aerial photography, alone as I wished to be.

Suddenly a thought emerged. In my mind I saw Violet. It appeared she was talking to me. I tried to concentrate my thoughts but too much was going on inside my head right now. I wonder if she asked Whispering Wind to teach her telepathy. I know she was interested and I didn't have time to show her. That was my fault. I didn't take the time to spend with her and teach her, or at least familiarize her with it. Again I let an opportunity pass for no real reason. My heart was racing now with just the thought of conversing with her. Eventually everything faded like a mist and I was alone again.

"Back to my photos," I said aloud trying to rationalize my

past neglect.

The next hour or so, I truly don't know how long, I spent looking at the air photos but not seeing anything. My mind was elsewhere. More heart than mind I would say. I needed to clear my head and my photos were not doing it. I grabbed my camera and went looking for Mario. I truly needed and wanted the distraction.

"Mr. Blue where are you ? " I laughed.

It was not too long before I found Mario. He appeared to welcome my company. Believe it or not I was able to help him in his recording work. In doing so I know I was helping myself.

I was satisfied with the rest of my day and Mario's company and at the same time we accomplished some serious recording work.

While walking back to camp speaking of nothing but trivial things Mario surprised me. In a subdued manner he casually asked, not expecting an answer.

"Is your mind settled down now so you can return to doing what you do best."

I shyly gazed at him and saw barely a grin. I looked away, grinning myself, and mentally said "Thank you."

He instantly replied without looking at me, "You re welcome."

~ ~ ~ ~ ~ ~

It was four thirty, Mario and I were working on supper when we saw our three companions exiting the temple and starting toward us. Drawing closer you could tell they were beat.

"I never knew walking could be so boring," Diego complained with a sad face.

Carlos reached the table and sat down sighing.

"Oh boy, does that feel good."

Mateo also chimed in,

"I bet we walked two hundred miles today."

"More like four hundred," Diego added.

$\mathbf{M}$ario and I served our hikers some fresh coffee, and soon after Mario announced dinner. Our three pals were ravenous. They finished their plates before Mario and I got to sit down. Luckily there was plenty to go around for the three walkers helped themselves to seconds.

$\mathbf{C}$arlos apparently sated now started to speak seriously.

"$\mathbf{Y}$ou were right Eric. There was absolutely nothing to see. You were right about the air ducts also. I tried to study what I could, but to no avail. That will have to wait until I have time to do some reverse engineering. The Glyph was again different. I had not seen it before. None of us had. Perhaps it was designed specifically for the tunnel vents."

"$\mathbf{I}$ suppose that's possible." I answered. "Look at us." I laughed. "A couple of rock diggers trying to out guess an advanced culture of hundreds, if not thousands of years old."

$\mathbf{C}$arlos smiled at my remark.

"$\mathbf{I}$ could not agree more, my friend."

"$\mathbf{H}$ow far do you think you traveled today ?" I inquired.

"$\mathbf{I}$ didn't do any exact measurements, but I think a good educated guess would be between eight and ten miles."

"$\mathbf{C}$loser to ten I would wager," volunteered Mateo.

"$\mathbf{T}$hat's even more than I expected." I replied. "Nice going, I will gauge about that amount on the aerial photography and see if I can discern anything. There has to be an entrance someplace."

"$\mathbf{R}$emember what I said," Carlos brought up. "Our ancients were masters at hiding, even cities."

"$\mathbf{B}$elieve it or not I know the truth of that now." I replied. "Nevertheless it won't hurt to try."

$\mathbf{E}$xcept for the Glyphs marking the fresh air stations there was nothing to report or talk about. It had been a rather dull, boring unexciting day. The conversation then turned to the two Spaniards whose body's had been there for hundreds of years. What should be done? The discussion went on for almost an hour. We finally agreed on a plan. Pictures would be taken and the bodies would be properly buried. Any personal papers would be returned to Spain after copies were made. All principal facts would be involved in a report to the Department of Antiquities, eventually including the tunnel. It was also agreed there was no hurry to fulfill these decisions. Just before turning in for the night I mentioned I wanted to walk the tunnel again. That discussion was active and quick. The others would decide by morning who would accompany me. I didn't want to say I would rather go alone because I did not want to hurt their feelings. I realized they were only looking out for my welfare.

As I lay there listening to my music I was also explaining the last few days to Dove of Spring. I know it sounds silly but it made me feel better sharing. Who knows ? Perhaps that will be my future.

~ ~ ~ ~ ~ ~ ~

The next thing I remember is my not so favorite Howler monkey alarm clock screeching me awake. They appeared to be louder than usual this morning. It was not just me being awakened. It seems the monkeys felt that everybody should be up and about.

"One of these days we're going to have monkey stew for dinner." Mario mumbled.

"And I'm going to enjoy every minute of it," added Diego.

There was the expected laughter, then Carlos reminded us,

"Do you have any ideas how many of those howlers are out there. We don't have that much ammunition."

After breakfast I started to gather my things together, at least what I thought I would need. Of course my camera was number one. Water, lunch, lantern and a normal sized hunting knife. I decided to take my GPS. I know it most likely would not work underground but it made me feel less lost, if that makes any sense. I was making sure that all was neatly packed in my small back pack when Diego approached followed by the other three.

"We drew straws and I lost so I'm going with you." claimed Diego.

I looked up into four smiling faces.

"Thanks guys for your vote of confidence. It's so nice to have such faithful support."

Carlos explained that it had to be Diego in order to protect the monkey population.

In another fifteen minutes Diego and I were wished good luck as we stepped into the tunnel.

Chapter 9

We set a good pace right from the beginning since the first part of this journey was surveyed twice. I was happy to have Diego with me. His free and easy personality reminded me of Lone Buffalo. No wonder they got along so well in college. They were like two peas in a pod. Conversation was always easy with Diego.

Once we passed the point I had reached the first day we slowed our travel slightly yet keeping a good gait. My point was to cover as much mileage as possible. We made no stops. Diego had no complaint about the pace we were keeping. It sure beat walking long distance in the desert sand. For whatever reason I thought of Whispering Wind and the walking pace he set that Dan and I had trouble keeping up with. We should have him walking the tunnel. We would probably be at the end already. I laughed to myself.

I tried the GPS to no avail, nor did I expect any results. I decided to keep trying every now and then. On my fourth try it did register a position. How accurate the readings were I could not ascertain. I had nothing to gauge it against. Leaving the GPS on I resumed walking and within four paces it went blank.

"Diego." I said "Look at this." as I showed him the instrument. We moved backward a little when suddenly the GPS registered the Lat and Lon again. A logical answer escaped us both. We stepped forward again. I did not want to lose any more time.

Twenty minutes further the GPS registered again and with different numbers. We stopped our forward motion with me now totally confused.

"There has to be an explanation," Diego said. "Perhaps it has to do with these Glyph's on the wall. I noticed there was one the last time it registered."

"That's got to be it. These Glyphs indicate air passages, which is why we can breath so easily down here. For what ever reason it's allowing a reading. But even that doesn't make any sense. We can't see or have direct line of sight with any satellites."

I recorded the numbers from the GPS anyway.

We kept going, picking up the pace somewhat. I wanted to gain ground, not lose it. Sure enough at the next Glyph I registered Lat and Lon Surprisingly they tied into previous logging's.

" I may get something out of this yet," I mentioned to Diego. "But I have no idea why."

He just laughed and advised, "Don't look a gift horse in the mouth."

I laughed along as we kept on moving.

It was just after one PM when we agreed we were both hungry. I suggested we eat while walking. I did not want to lose time. Being a good sport, knowing how much this meant to me, Diego had no objections.

We continued on at the physically torturing pace. At four PM Diego reminded me that perhaps we should go back. As it is we wouldn't be back before dark I gave that some thought but something inside of me said "Keep Going". I stopped, turned and looked at Diego.

"Don't take this the wrong way my friend, you may go back if you choose, but I'm going to continue. I'm far too excited to quit at this point. I still have water and food and a spare light source. I will not be angry with you if you choose to return. There was a moment of silence then Diego spouted.

"Ah what the heck, I'll share you're glory with you."

I genuinely smiled and was happy he chose to go on. We turned and resumed our rapid tread. We had exhausted another forty minutes and as we turned a slight bend we were startled by another Conquistador lying face down with three arrows in his back. He still held on to his sword which was stained. It had obviously just been used before he himself was killed. I stopped and captured everything on film while Diego went through the personal belongings.

We started our walk again and only traveled about one hundred feet when we came upon the decayed corps of a local native, obviously Mayan by the way he was attired. Diego offered his prayers to the deceased ancestor and I gladly joined him.

Underway once more I posed to Diego...

"After finding these two fine soldiers I wouldn't be surprised there will be an entrance somewhere in the area."

Diego smiled, "If you sense it, I would not at all be surprised to find one."

I smiled in answer but kept on walking.

Eventually we came upon another Glyph so naturally I took another GPS reading and logged it with the rest. Not only did I get the Lat and Lon but for some reason the altitude was also recording and we were definitely on an up hill climb. If the altimeter was now registering, it struck me as a possibility that the overhead of the tunnel was becoming less dense. On a whim I asked Diego to be on the lookout for an entrance or opening. There may be something here or nearby. Diego again just smiled but started to seriously pay attention.   I thought the resemblance of personalities between he and Dan or Lone Buffalo was amazing.

It couldn't have been more than fifteen or twenty minutes when we both noticed a change in the tunnel structure. The walls and ceiling were suddenly not as smooth as they had been, particularly the overhead. We moved slowly and carefully checking every foot we traveled. Abruptly there was a change again. As the tunnel continued everything had a finished appearance once more. Even the floor was less rough. I made Diego aware of my suspicions that an outside entrance may exist in that rough walled area. He agreed, although with less conviction then I expected, with my assessment. We proceeded with a more careful scrutiny. Down deep inside I was straining my wishes that there was a portal to the outside world.

"I told you my friend, you need not my help in the discovery of things you wish to find."

The king's message was unexpected but it confirmed for me   my highest hopes.   It wasn't long after the kings words of encouragement that an excited Diego drew my attention to a section of the wall that was slightly indented and extremely uneven. from the rest.

"Nice going Diego," I complimented as I viewed the wall in question.   On closer inspection I came upon what looked like loose stones.   Sure enough they were easily moved. Diego wisely suggested that only one of us work in the loose stone area in case of a sudden cave in.   His logic made sense and he insisted he be the one to pull at the stones.   I chose not to argue with him.   I knew his heart was in the right place.

Just as Diego moved to the stone wall I hurriedly cautioned.

"Wait, don't go near the wall !"

Diego stopped and turned to me with a frightened expression.

"I'm sorry my friend, I didn't mean to alarm you."

"What's the problem ?" he asked.

"I may be over reacting but look at the wall.   There's no order to those stones.   By that I mean the way they are laid out.   Also look at the floor.   There is an awful lot of dirt and dust and small rock chips."

"As if there was a cave in." Diego muttered in agreement.

"Exactly." I answered.   "Possibly a cave in on purpose."

You could see the light go on in Diego's mind.

"They were finished with the cave and filled in the entrance, just like the place we were digging back by the tomb."

"Right again.   At least that's my way of thinking."

"I believe you're correct.   If we start to dig this out we would end up under this rock pile."   He added with a smile.   "Then we would most likely miss dinner."

Forever the clown but I had to laugh along with him. We stood there quietly staring at the wall for the longest time.

"Well ! " I finally spoke, "That leaves us back to walking some more.   I still say we go forward."

"Lead on "Oh Hunter of Stories," Diego smiled.

"Right then he sounded like Lone Buffalo' I thought.

Each of us automatically grabbed a snack from our pack

and munched while walking. Before we realized it was six o'clock. I made it a point to stop at the next Glyph.

"We know it's too late to turn back and I don't think we will be expected. Early this morning I mentioned to Carlos that depending on what we do or do not find I may keep on going, so they shouldn't worry too much."

"Not to worry." Diego replied. "I figured it was something like that otherwise you would have turned back a long tome ago."

"Are you tired ? Do you want to rest ?" I asked.

"Naaa, let's see where this leads."

We were on our way once again.

We traveled for another two hours seeing nothing new. The only thing that was new was really old. New to us, yet actually hundreds of years old. We stopped at the next Glyph we came upon because of the air vent. Here we decided to rest and/or sleep. We sat down, backs against a wall and totally relaxed. I have to admit the pace we kept up all day positively drained our strength. We did not realize how much until we stopped. We looked at each other, out of breath, and laughed.

"I guess this is where we rest for a while," I said in general.

"And maybe even get some sleep for about three days or so." added Diego.

"I guess that's not a bad idea." I replied smiling. "How far do you think we have traveled ?"

"Oh I don't know, I would estimate about two hundred miles with the way my legs feel. That is when I can feel them." Diego laughed again in response. "Seriously though I would say in the neighborhood of twenty."

"Yeah, I would guestimate that also. How are you fixed for food ?"

"Actually I think I'm alright. I needed to lose a little weight anyway."

I chuckled along with Diego again then posed. "I have this gut feeling that our next trek will lead us to our destination."

"Which is ?" quizzed Diego.

"An entrance, or exit, depending on how you want to look

at it. I even brought along some of the aerials of a point of interest I had seen. Which is where I hope we come out."

"**I**'m with you pal. Perhaps we should ask Atal for some help."

"We could," I answered. "But I would rather wait until tomorrow or whenever it is we reach an exit."

"**I** have no problem with that." Diego replied now almost totally stretched out on the floor with his pack as a pillow.

Sleep, very easily took over both would be explorers. The days exhaustive pace finally reaped it's toll and demanded payment.

I sensed movement and opened my eyes to see Diego stretching his stiff body.

"**W**hat time is it." I mumbled in a sleepy voice.

"**M**y watch says five o seven."

"**O**oooooo" I replied.

Diego smiled warmly as he offered "Bacon, eggs, toast and coffee are almost ready, or if you prefer, your choice of energy bar."

I answered in kind; "I think I would prefer the energy bar today. The coffee just keeps me awake."

It took about twenty minutes to stretch out the kinks and eat something but we were raring to go. It wasn't too long after resuming our trek that we both noticed we were walking a slight incline. I didn't say anything in particular to Diego, but my hopes were high for an exit soon. Having walked patiently for close to two hours we soon came upon a crude set of steps. We were both elated about this having had enough of walking in a basement atmosphere.

We stopped to give this some thought. Could we or could we not open this to the outside world or was it sealed in such a way only to be opened from topside. We rested while we debated our problem.

"**T**o start with," Diego posed. "Only one of us at a time should check out the stairway. For safety sake." he smiled.

*"**T**here's that Lone Buffalo look again."*

Diego volunteered to go first. I wasn't going to argue with him and take away his fun. We discussed what to look for based on our history of our finds so far. He was like a little kid starting an adventure. I know the feeling well, having been through it many times both here and in the desert.

I stepped back as he started up the stone steps just in case of a fall out from above. Diego was only up about twenty five feet when he called to me.

"I can't go any further. There appears to be a flat platform, but I can't budge it. I'm coming down."

Once down he looked frustrated but yet excited.

"You were right, this is obviously an entrance."

"But." I interrupted him, "We have to remember it has not been used for at least four hundred years. I would imagine the earth is pretty well compacted by now. Let me have a look."

I carefully climbed the stairs, lantern in hand. When I could go no further I carefully studied the overhead platform.

"There has to be a handle or lever or something," I thought.

I spent about fifteen minutes looking but with no success. I gave up for the time being returning to Diego. I explained what I had done and suggested while resting we continue down the tunnel. He agreed and also suggested that we both go up the steps. He felt there was room for two. I thought of the space and concurred with him. Perhaps the two of us could manage something together.

In ten minutes they happened upon what was obviously the end of the tunnel. There were no longer smooth rock surfaces. Everything ended as rubble. There was a suspicious section they guessed was at one time an egress to the above world. It too was filled with debris and small rocks and jungle waist. Feeling good that this was the tunnel's end they gingerly walked back to what they hoped was the exit.

As discussed earlier the two carefully climbed the stairs at the same time looking for a hidden key or latch. Once as high as they could go they took extra care in looking for a trigger device, fingers becoming raw from the rough edges of stone. After some twenty minutes of touching and feeling, a click, or rather a muffled thump was heard. It came from a side ninety degrees to the steps.

Diego and I looked at each other smiling. I raised both arms to lift at that edge of the platform. Knowing this probably had not been opened for hundreds of years I put some effort into my push. Nothing moved, but there were a few chips of stone that fell from the edge. With that incentive I tried both arms in an upward push. There was some movement though it was ever so slight. I held my upward push as long as I could then dropped my arms to rest and catch my breath. I gave myself a few moments then turned to Diego. I did not have to use words, my request showed in my eyes. He smiled and moved up next to me. I nodded and we both pushed upward. With an extra effort from both of us we raised the platform a few inches. We finally let go. As the platform shut there was again a small shower of dirt and stone chips. We both sported broad grins now and rested. Words were not necessary, we knew what we had to do.
I found a large stone which had a span of about five inches yet was light enough to handle with one hand. I set it into position close to the platform. Again we both lifted, high enough to get the spacer stone in place. That extra push on our part earned us a rest.

We returned to the tunnel floor, sat and snacked while resting.

"This is really something Eric. We all read fables of tunnels used to hide treasure from the Spaniards, but no one has ever found one. So the legends went on to truly become just that, "Legends" They became folk lore for many people. Now we're sitting in one."

Diego was truly excited by this.

Smiling and happy to see my friend so excited I casually remarked,

"And these legends have these tunnels throughout South America, North America and even into Canada. It sounds like a whole subterranean culture."

I was almost laughing by the time I finished my comments. True, we had just found a tunnel but that did not make us a full believer that they were throughout the whole of the western hemisphere. We both appeared to be rested so I suggested we go back to the exit. Diego was all for the idea and was on his feet before I was halfway up.

"Come on old man, a little work will do you good."

"Watch it there young one, you're supposed to have respect for your elders," I scolded.

At the foot of the steps we stopped to give some thought as to a logical plan of attack.

"The one wedge we put in," I started, "Seemed to do the job."

Before I could continue Diego jumped right in.

"So if we were to keep putting wedges in, you know larger and larger, perhaps that would work."

"I agree Diego, but there is an unknown."

"And what's that." he asked.

"We have no idea what's on top of the platform. I suspect it's more than a few inches of dirt."

Diego smiled, almost laughing, "I hate it when people always think of the small details. You're right of course. So what do you suggest ?"

"That's the problem or suggestion, I don't have any ideas. I believe what you just outlined is probably the best bet," I smiled.

I sort of mumbled to myself, "Where are you Mr. Blue when I need you ?"

Diego heard me and expressed his own thoughts.

"I was just thinking the same thing. I remember the stories you told about your spider friend."

Diego repeated my thoughts out loud. "Where are you Mr. Blue ?"

I chuckled somewhat and when I did Diego turned to look at me. I answered his questioning eyes with this;

"I was just thinking how we would react if he showed right now." And he laughed along with me as we started up the steps.

We were able to raise the platform up another couple of inches and fit another stone in to hold its position. Over the next ten minutes we were able to do this three more times, which allowed us an opening of just over a foot. Satisfied with the apparent progress we were making I descended the stairs to get another wedge stone. With my back to the steps and bending to grasp the stone I heard a terrible rumble. Before

I could look up various sized rocks knocked me to the ground. It was then I heard an even more terrible and louder roar of stone and rubble partially burying me. I tried moving but a heavier load pushed me flat. As flat as one could be laying on a pile of uneven rocks.

Suddenly there was silence. Eery silence. A stillness unknown to me before. It took me a few moments to regain my awareness of what just occurred.

Surprisingly I was still able to move, only when I did I found unexpected pain. Flashbacks of being buried alive back in the desert ran through my mind. Slowly collecting my thoughts I cried out Diego's name. I received no answer. I called out louder. Still no answer. Thoughts I did not want flashed through my mind. I took a deep breath in an attempt to settle myself. I waited and took a few more deep breaths and then attempted to move again. I was able to move my right arm slightly. I realized my limited movement was due to the piles of rock on top of me. I exercised my fingers which luckily worked without too much of a problem. Using my right arm for leverage I tried pushing my body up. As I did so I could feel the points of rocks and rubble pushing into my back, but there was movement, painful though it was, which encouraged me to try harder. My left arm was now free and the movement process indicated there were no broken bones. One by one I slowly moved each of my legs. The muscles hurt like hell with the movement, but again , proved to me anyway, that there were no severely broken bones. Hopefully not broken at all. I struggled and rested, struggled and rested until at last my legs were totally free. I never before realized what the freedom of movement meant. It seemed to free my mind also.

I instantly turned to find Diego. I did not care about my stiffness or bruising, I immediately started clearing stone and debris away. It didn't take too much time when I could finally see his arm and hand. Using this as a guide I cleared away rubble searching for his head. Once the head and shoulders were cleared I checked his pulse. It was steady, weaker than I thought it should be, but steady nonetheless. Retrieving my canteen I splashed water on his face. It took some doing with water drips till I saw my efforts rewarded. His head moved slightly as he opened his eyes ever so hesitantly.

"Hi there sleepy." I said with a big smile. "Don't move yet." I cautioned. "Can you feel your body ?"

"It hurts like hell, so I guess I'm feeling it." he replied slowly trying to smile.

"I guess that's as good a sign as any." I said attempting to keep my voice on an up note. "Don't go any where." I joked. "I'm going to start clearing away the mess you made in my tunnel."

Picking up on my attempt at levity he answered with,

"I thought it was our tunnel, therefore, this is our mess."

"Okay." I laughed, "But I already cleaned up my half of the mess. I'll start cleaning yours now."

As I was talking I was already moving the rocks. It wasn't long before I had him totally exposed.

"Okay, my friend, I'm going to check for broken bones. Try not to cry too much."

He laughed but understood what I meant. I did not take long, Diego was even able to help somewhat even though I discouraged it. With effort from both of us we managed to get him free and clear. He was now lying on his back, his pack as a pillow totally free from the rock fall.

"You are very lucky my friend." I explained. I can only see minor bleeding at the moment."

"That's good. I can't stand the sight of blood, especially my own." joked Diego

"BUT" I said a little more seriously. I am going to check you out completely."

I proceeded with a total examination of him.

"Minor cuts and bruises was all I found till I got to his left leg. There was no blood but when I moved it slowly he winced with pain and cried out. I cut open his trousers to examine closer. I am far from being a doctor but it did not take much to figure nothing was broken but his knee was dislocated. I dared not go any further with my exam. He needed more help than I could provide and we both knew it.

"Okay Diego we have two options. First, I run, or go as fast as I can back and get the others, which will take many, many hours with you here alone. Or secondly I rig up what I can and drag your sorry bones for help which would be half the time. I'm saying this because I don't want to leave you out of the decision. I know what my preference is but I would like to hear from you."

Diego was quiet but moving his body. Then looking at me with a grin replied, "Well, I don't think I'm hurt as bad as we both thought a little while ago. I say we go out together."

I smiled while nodding my head saying, "Good."

Diego continued, "If you leave me here alone, I'd probably start crying for my mommy and then I would not get my ice cream cone today. " He laughed.

"Okay." I laughed with him. "A minute ago I saw you trying to move. How much can you move ?"

"Good question, let's find out," he cheerfully answered.

He started with his arms, gingerly. I kept my eyes on his face to detect any pain. First one arm then the other to the point where he was moving them freely.

"Some discomfort, but I wouldn't call it pain," he replied.

"Now the right leg."

First he turned his foot left and right, then pulled the knee up towards his chest. I could tell by his eyes he was not that comfortable, but he persisted with the bandaged knee exercise some what improved. He looked at me again, definite questions showing. Even turning the foot took its toll on his face.

"Don't go any further." I cautioned. "We both know that's not going to work. Okay, now we know what we have to do."

"We do ?" Diego joked again,

I smiled and turned away from him toward the exit mess. I thought I remembered seeing some tree limbs and pieces of vine among the rubble. I was correct, now I just had to find out how much and how useful. I looked over my shoulder and it appeared Diego was comfortable for the moment. I went to work.

After about an hour or so of moving stone I had pile of junk in front of me. The majority of the tree limbs were only four to five feet long, too short to make a proper litter. But I told myself there are plenty of small pieces. Ideas began to flow in my head about how to piece things together and for the next hour and a half I worked non stop. I used our trouser belts and pack straps for rope. I tore strips from our shirts and used our sox. All went to the cause of securing this collection of sticks together. At long last I had a dragging litter made from the hodge podge of junk.

Diego and I just about finished the last of our food supply. After a short rest we were at last ready to go. Diego was of great help to me in getting him secured on to the litter.

"Wait !" Diego yelled. "Did we at least get the platform open ?"

I gazed at him questioning his sanity at this moment.

"Who cares." I commented. "Right now the important thing is you."

"Could you at least look." He then added "Please" with a grin. I smiled back shaking my head.

"Okay, okay." I replied walking back to the exit. I returned in a few minutes.

"Well" he insistently questioned.

"I couldn't really tell with all that rock. I couldn't even find the steps." I smiled.

Diego appeared to be disappointed and that I understood.

I slipped my shoulders into the pulling straps and we were on our way. The initial start was slow and difficult, but as the drag of the pulling on the stone floor smoothed out the support sticks the pull became easier. I stopped about every thirty minutes to rest.

"Do you want to lie down for a while and I'll pull ?" Diego clowned.

"Keep joking like that and I just may let you," I smiled in answer.

The hours passed by slowly, my pace becoming slower. Let's face it I was tired. But my concern for Diego drove me on. I felt my mind wander and suddenly precious words appeared. *"Return To Me"* I know it may sound silly but my energy and strength were renewed. I forged on as if I had just started. I finally and knowingly declared my commitment to Dove of Spring. I was happy with my decision. I was smiling both inwardly and outwardly as I trekked on.

I figured there was about at least three hours to go when I heard voices. Familiar voices.

"Over here, we're coming," I yelled excitedly. I could now hear running footsteps. A few more seconds and I saw Carlos and Mario.

I stopped and let them run to me. I figured they were probably feeling fresher than I was. Diego, being himself of course greeted them.

"**H**ey you guys, you missed all the fun and if you help me back to camp I'll tell you all about it. Besides the driver of this rig is going too slow."

You couldn't help but laugh with him and at him.

The rest of my walk was much easier now that I didn't have to drag the sled. By the time we got to camp we had related the whole story to Carlos and Mario. Mateo was equally pleased to see us.

Carlos from his earlier days coaching high school football had seen many dislocated knees. He felt confident he could reset Diego's who readily agreed for him to do it. Carlos was successful on the first attempt though not without pain which Diego handled quite well considering the circumstances.

Food for both of us was next on our list and then a good rest in our comfy hammocks.

I guess our trek through the tunnel and back took a greater toll on me than I thought. Once I got to my hammock and made myself comfortable I said good night to Violet and let my symphony take me. It took me away without dreams. So much so that I slept like a rock through the night and part of the morning. It was well after nine when I tumbled out of my hammock. It was almost like taking the potion from Sky Above the Mountain back with my Navajo friends. I have to admit though, that uninterrupted sleep was just what the doctor ordered. My muscles were a bit sore yet I felt like a million bucks, or at least a thousand bucks.

As I approached the table I got the usual ribbing I expected for sleeping so late. My first concern of course was Diego but there he was joking with the rest as if nothing had occurred over the last two days. The coffee was extra good this morning and I was surprised at how hungry I was. While eating we discussed the two remains we came across in the tunnel. Proper services and burial would be shown as with the others.

More questions were put forth to us about the possible entrance we found, of course I was anxious to go back there but this time it

would be above ground. I only hoped we could find the right location.
Carlos questioned whether or not I could locate it. I agreed it was just a shot
in the dark, but with a guestimate of miles we covered and the basic
direction we traveled I had high hopes I could identify something from the
aerial photography. I did mention that I had recorded the GPS positions by
the air vent areas. With any luck and keeping my fingers crossed as to their
accuracy they would be of great assistance to my plotting. Diego
volunteered to help me with the guess work in our plotting. That was our
assignment for the day while the other three continued their routine work.
This also allowed Diego and myself another day of recuperation which we
were both thankful for.

As the others left camp Diego and I turned our attention to
the map table. Constant consultation with Diego between mugs of coffee
and I felt I was making headway. I sat back letting my mind rerun its
memory scan of the tunnel.

***"Your dedication to this work is a wonderful
thing my friend, although it does not surprise me."***

I was momentarily startled at hearing Atal's voice. I was
not expecting it.

***"It is also no surprise to me that you are on the
right track. Stay the course you are following and you will
find your end result."***

"But what will I find and what am I looking for." I asked
not expecting a reply. I was right in my feeling the king was no longer
there. You would think I would be used to this by now I repeated to myself
again, and again and again it seemed.

I took a quick glance at Diego and detected no reaction.
"Good" I thought, *"The king excluded him from that short
conversation. I keep asking myself what am I looking for ? The king
appears to know and that puts him one up on me."*
Diego brought me back to reality when he raised his head

from the stereo glasses and with his usual joking manner remarked,

"I don't know how you do what you do with this stuff I see nothing but jungle tree tops resulting in getting my eyes crossed and giving me a headache."

I laughed as he slid the glasses and photo's back to me.

"Okay" I replied. "You continue to work on mileage distance and I'll plot your results along with the GPS readings. That should result in something."

Diego's recall was obviously better than mine. He even remembered the turns we took, their approximate angles and the distance between. Maybe it has to do with that artist recall.

A short time later I reviewed our combined efforts and low and behold we had an actual plot that aligned itself with my interpretation squiggles on the air photo's. I was suddenly filled with excitement once again.

"Now my friend," I muttered addressing Diego. "We just have to walk this line we have created to verify its accuracy. Personally I don't have any doubts it will bear out our findings."

Diego was all smiles again.

"When do we start." he voiced with extreme animation.

"Whoa ! Back it down my friend. Common sense dictates we wait another day. Let's face it, we just went through a rough couple of days. Another day of rest will not hurt either of us. I'm also sure our three other companions would insist on it."

Looking slightly dejected Diego agreed with my thinking. You could tell he was restless and eventually wandered off with a folding chair and his sketch pad. I turned my attention back to fine tune my tunnel track above ground. The rest of the day seemed to drag. Both Diego and I knew we had to rest and recuperate but that did nothing to cool down our excitement of the search we knew was waiting for us. I could not wait to walk this path to the jungle entrance.

Chapter 10

We were like overexcited children when our three companions returned to camp. We really needed the extra stimulation to finally break up our more than boring day.

I usually look forward to alone time, yet being this close to finding the answer to another mystery left me at a loss not being able to follow through when I wanted to. It was the first time in years I felt that I was not in control. Knowing I was being foolish for feeling this way made me even more upset with myself.

Trying to act calm I slowly inquired about their day pretending a great interest in their recorded paper work. It took a few minutes till I finally eased my self built tension. Things felt normal once again as talk of dinner preparations took priority.

During dinner Diego and I spoke of what we thought of as success in laying out the tunnel trail above ground. Diego went on to emphasize the possibility of determining the secret of the air vents. This was something we all thought of that could be of great interest to engineers of today. Our hopes were running high.

Our relaxing but exciting dinner over we went our separate ways for journal updating and rest. With my symphonic background and my comfy hammock, mosquito netting and all, my thoughts drifter to Violet.. Actually they did not drift, I wanted to talk with her. My eyes closed as I pictured her the first night I took her to dinner. The highlights in her raven black hair and beautiful buckskin dress highlighted her classic beauty. Not realizing it. I silently called out her Navajo name. The words seemed to hang there as if floating with the jungle serenade.

"I am here my love. I will always be here for you."

I was startled at hearing her voice. Were we actually communicating or was it just my wishful thinking.

"This wish belongs to both of us,"

came my answer. I bolted upright in my hammock only to hear a fading,

"Return to me."

I immediately closed my eyes again listening intently. It was too late. Our connection had been severed and I knew it would be futile to try and reestablish. My jungle music alone would have to suffice for the night. I could feel myself smile. I was once again content and happy as sleep took over.

~ ~ ~ ~ ~ ~

I awoke the same way I went to sleep, thoughts of Violet filling my head. I lay there enjoying my visions until the howlers decided I had enough. I enjoyed their wake up calls for the longest time but lately I found them to be most intrusive. I laughed at myself remembering I'm the one intruding on their domain. I silently wished them a good morning as I slowly dragged myself to my feet. A quick wash up and I made my way to the coffee pot. Carlos was up and already had made the coffee. I silently thanked him as I filled my brown stained mug.

"So today's the big day," he said as an opening remark.

"I hope so. I put an awful lot of wishing into it so far."

"I really believe you will find your opening but I won't be going with you today." Carlos said sadly.

"I'm sorry to hear that," I returned sincerely. "I understand how important you're recording work is and I thoroughly concur with your decision."

He smiled replying that wasn't the reason.

"**I** should be continuing with that but you got me thinking last night of the other underground structure that you and I discovered our first season here. So while you and Diego see your efforts to a conclusion I'm going to take Mateo with me and do some preliminary study of that trapezoidal temple."

"**I** would love to do that with you but right now finding that tunnel entrance needs my full attention."

"**I** also understand where you are coming from in that regard. Once you find your entrance and get it recorded you can join me and use your special talent to discover something new for us."

"**Y**ou have just renewed my excitement. No wonder we all love this place so much. There is always something new behind each tree."

Eric sought out Diego to discuss what their plan should be and what to take with them.

"**E**xtra food this time. Those energy bars are okay once in a while but they really don't fill the stomach." smiled Diego.

"**M**y thoughts exactly, my friend. As long as we have real food available let's take advantage. I've had enough experience of going without."

The rest of our list was pretty standard; machete, shovel, lantern, GPS, air photo's and camera naturally. We knew it would be a long day, perhaps two days. Walking the jungle would not be as easy as the unobstructed tunnel.

As much as I wanted to get an early start it was well after nine thirty by the time we were on our way. Using the GPS we followed the plot we established on the air photo's. It was slow going, slower than I originally figured. Once we were out of sight of the pyramid the jungle was more dense than I could have imagined. The machete slashing kept Diego and I both busier than expected. It was more stressful than those past explorations. I realized, too late of course, that we probably should have given ourselves at least one more day of rest, yet neither of us wanted to turn back.

We forged on through the aches and discomfort keeping to our plotted route. Again I must compliment Diego on his memory of the turns and distances of our tunnel trek. Everything was matching pretty well to my original pencil dots on the photography.

We eventually made it to the first recorded, what we called an air vent area. Of course we stopped and did a quick search for an above ground hint of an air supply system. Absolutely nothing was apparent. My first thinking was we would have to wait for Carlos and his expertise on hidden history. I could not believe how anxious I was to get to the tunnel end. Here I was passing up an opportunity to research an air vent system that could possibly be of great benefit to all mankind only because I wanted to find the entrance that we already knew existed and was not going to move elsewhere.

"Hold up Diego. We know the tunnel entrance exists and we know approximately where."

"That's true and I have the scars to prove it," joked Diego in answer. "So what's your point ?"

Looking directly at him I explained.

"Let's apply the proper attention to conduct a true search for the air vents."

Diego smiled in agreement.

"Good," he whispered as he sat on the ground. "I really need a rest."

"Again, you have showed your true self, Eric. Ever the scientist. Leave the discovery of the obvious to those who do not possess your passion."

I immediately turned to Diego who was resting his weary muscles. He gave no indication of disturbance by the king.

"My words are for you only Eric."

"Can you help me ?" I pleaded.

"You always seek help when it is unnecessary."

"**B**ut where do I start ? At least give me that much."

"The air way you seek, as always, rides on the wind."

"**A**gain with the riddles," I answered annoyed though I knew the king was no longer there.

Turning my attention back to Diego I asked.

"**H**ow are you feeling ?"

"**B**elieve it or not that short rest did me a world of good."

"**I** can't disagree on that, I feel better myself." I replied

Diego, with that quirky expression he sometimes has, smiled up at me asking.

"**Y**ou were just in contact with the king, weren't you ?"

"**Y**ou could tell that easily ?" I asked.

"**Y**eah, I'm getting used to your frustration faces."

I laughed along with him verbalizing my annoyance out loud.

"**H**e's speaking in his usual riddle language again."

"**T**ell me," Diego replied cheerfully. "Perhaps between the two of us we can work it out."

There was that contagious Lone Buffalo smile again, but it did cure my annoyance with the king.

I repeated verbatim the kings words.

"The air way you seek, as always, rides on the wind."

Diego thought for a while, then gazing directly at me voiced his frustration also.

"**Y**ou're right. He does like riddles."

Trying hard not to let it get to us too much we slowly walked around the approximate area again while letting our minds analyze the riddle. This mental telepathy thing turned out to be quite a gift and Diego and I took advantage of it every chance we got. More so I think than with the others.

While we meandered around slashing we would each make a suggestion, most of which were nixed by the other. This enabled us to search uninterrupted, separate areas without having to go back and forth to look or talk about something.

We eventually did meet up again after an unsuccessful attempt of seeking what we did not know. Wow! Talk about riddles.

Yet baffled by the king's words we sat down on a fallen tree.

"Speaking of riddles." Diego pulled out of thin air with that contagious grin.

"Now what ?" I asked as I turned to him sporting my own smile

"While thinking of the kings riddle, it just dawned on me why the riddles."

I remained with my eyes fixed on him but they were now questioning.

"Remembering my ancient studies of the "Popol Vuh"*, Riddles were in common use in the beginning by the sovereign leaders, Gods, Kings or what ever. It was a way of teaching, making one think in detail, etc."

I'll have to admit it suddenly made sense to me.

"Now where was I ?----Oh yeah."

"What rides on the wind ?"

"Nothing but dirt, dust and leaves," chided Diego. "And my final term paper out an open window during my senior year in college." he added with a smile.

Silence once again. Then a sudden mutual outcry, **"Leaves"** and after a slight pause another mutual **"Trees."**

We were both on our feet now looking up. I checked the GPS once again in order to pinpoint the spot as exact as possible. We both moved to that position. Diego mentioned that when in the tunnel I was

---

* The Holy Book of the Maya

standing in the middle not near the wall. His memory really amazes me. Of course he was right. If I recall properly the overhead of the tunnel was solid. There was no obvious holes or vents or cracks of any kind. So how was the air entering the underground cavern ? Diego verbalizing my thoughts commented.

"That is the million dollar question my friend."

We both exchanged frustrated looks once again. I remained at the exact GPS location while my young artist friend moved to where he thought the wall was. That particular spot, where the Glyph was on the wall was about twelve feet from me. Nothing was obvious to either of us. My stymied brain was allowing tension to build. That was the last thing I wanted or needed. I then aired aloud my unwanted defeat.

"This is ridiculous. What are we doing here ? Why, after almost five hundred years do we expect to find something still intact anyway ? We should really just go about excavating something that we can see and feel and know it exists.

Diego, in a slightly raised voice shut me down.

"Whoa there Eric. Listen to yourself. I have never known you to give up on anything, here and probably not in the desert either. This is not you talking. Let's take a break, sit down and have a snack. You really need to calm down."

Embarrassed now and feeling my face go crimson I did as Diego requested. After sitting I apologized directly to him, and now he was featuring his ever present smile.

"It's all forgotten now my friend but I do understand your frustration but to answer your own question, the air system must be working, we ourselves experienced it or would not be here right now."

Obviously he was correct. My own internal anger was clouding my logical thinking process.

"On that you are accurate Diego and I should have realized that before going off the deep end. The system is still working, but how and where ?"

"That is for us to discover. Isn't that why we are here ?"

I could feel myself returning to normal now, if I was ever normal to start with. Well at least I was back to my normal.

"Look directly in front of you, what you seek is there."

Diego was witness to these new words from the king and we grinned knowingly at each other. Neither of us attempted a follow up contact because we knew he had disconnected.

"All I see is trees and vines." said Diego declaring the obvious. "No matter which way I look."

We remained silent for a moment.

"Wait a minute," I whispered.

"I'll wait for as long as you want," clowned Diego.

"No, I'm serious," I declared. "I was just remembering last year when Carlos and I discovered that trapezoidal structure that was mostly underground."

"So what does that have to do with this," asked a puzzled Diego.

"It was surrounded by a wall of trees, some of them false, or at least not growing. They had been purposely put in between other living trees to make the wall impenetrable. You would never really know it unless you directly and closely inspected the living wall."

"So the living wall was half dead." jested Diego again.

I couldn't help but laugh with him.

Turning instantly serious, my clowning companion arose and voiced my thoughts again.

"We have to check for phony trees."

"That's a good a start as any," I replied.

Diego, eyes on the ground started searching the area.

"Why are you looking on the ground ?"

"This is why." he replied as he bent over and picked up a hefty stick. "A hollow tree will sound different from a growing one."

"You're not a stupid as you look," I mocked with a smile.

"Yeah, it is amazing isn't it," he razed himself.

Each now armed with a mallet stick we proceeded our tree thumping process. After what we perceived as a few false alarms we both heard a distinctive different sound on two different trees spaced about eight feet apart. Filled with all kinds of emotions, including a possible letdown, we decided to keep checking. Our hunch paid off as a third tree with a similar sounding thump was located. It was triangularly located approximately eight feet from our first find. Excited once again we stood there viewing our success, or what we hoped was success.

"You didn't happen to pack a ladder with you, did you ?" jested Diego once more.

"Of course I did, just not one that will reach thirty plus feet high."

"That's okay," he replied. "I'll just run down to the local hardware store. I'll be back in about a month."

We were both feeling childish with our clowning. But the fact was we now have another problem to overcome.

Still recovering from our cave in ordeal we sat down to ponder this new road block.

"We should try and approach this in a logical manner," stated Diego.

Taking a clue from his normal manner I replied.

"Well that lets both of us out."

Not expecting that from me, Diego burst out laughing. Both of us were laughing so hard we disturbed the serenity of the jungle. It seemed the unseen birds and monkeys joined in. This prolonged our own silliness but it did clear our minds.

"Now, back to what you were saying Diego ?"

"Oh yeah that. I was just trying to imagine how do you hollow out a tree that is twenty or thirty feet high, to allow air flow ?"

"Great question," I muttered. "Do you have the answer ?"

"If I had the answer I wouldn't have asked the question." he answered with a silly grin.

"Seriously though, not without modern equipment." he smiled.

There was a long pause of silence. Even the jungle noise ceased.

"We have to check out one of those trees we think is hollow."

"What are you thinking now ?" Diego inquired softly.

"**T**his may sound silly but what if it's not a hollow tree

" **I**f it's not hollow how does air flow through it ?"

" **W**hat I mean is, what if it's not a whole tree but only the outer bark ?"

The light of the idea suddenly hit Diego.

"**Y**ou may be on to something. I know for a fact that it is not too difficult to strip large sections of bark from some of these local trees. It has something to do with the dampness the trees hold from the heavy rains."

Both men stood at the same time. This idea they had to check out. Standing by one of the so called hollow trees Eric's directed his companion to use his knife to try and cut through the bark while he reached for his entrenching tool.

"**I**'m going to dig, if I can, at the base to see where it leads us."

They worked quietly meeting more resistance than they expected. The first few feet of digging was earth and debris. After that was a lot of stones used as fill with the dirt. This was discouraging yet encouraging at the same time. The stone backfill was apparently man made.

Diego's task of cutting through the bark was no easier. He was stumped at first, then realized the bark itself was partially coated with a mortar like substance which cried like modern day cement. He paused in his hacking and set into motion his artist mind to analyze the synthetic bark. It truly was a pliable mixture made to match the bark including added colors of various densities.

"**L**ook at this Eric." Diego yelled, only to be matched by a "Look at this Diego." that Eric shouted.

Agreeable smiles appeared as they let the telepathic abilities take over. Each impressed by the other's find they agreed a break was in order.

I drank deeply from my canteen while conducting a detailed search of the tree in question. It was a false tree supported upright by intertwined branches of nearby trees.

"**W**hat a unique idea." I thought and was agreed upon by

Diego.

They stood away somewhat gauging the diameter of the make believe jungle piece. Diego guessed about twenty inches. The actual inner dimension was yet to be determined.

Turning their attention to Eric's digging attempt they agreed it was man made back fill that most likely went all the way down to the actual tunnel.

"Secret solved," claimed Diego. "Yet it was no minor feat of inventiveness. Intriguing, isn't it."

"You're right." I replied. "The most intriguing part is the artificial bark reproduction. When you think about it though it really is no surprise. Look at all the other works of art your ancestors produced. Another visit to the tunnel will be necessary to see the actual entrance portal of the air.

"What say we head back to camp. If we leave now we can make it back just before dark. Finding the actual tunnel entrance we can leave for another day when we will have no interference," Diego posed in a very tired voice.

"I concur completely Diego. I hate to admit it but I'm beat. We should have taken that extra day of rest."

"That's what tomorrow will be for us. Lets go, we have a lot to tell the others."

Chapter 11

It was great to be back at camp. A welcoming home for us so to speak, we were truly exhausted. Of course we had no one to blame but ourselves for not taking that extra day to rest, though the excitement of our find appeared to make our efforts worthwhile.

Carlos and the others returned with Carlos and Mateo as excited as Diego and me.

"I don't know if I can handle all this additional excitement after the day I just went through," Mario said matter of factly.

We all looked at him with much concern and inquisitiveness. With a dry monotone voice he continued.

"While super busy with my recording work at one of the stelae, twice, not once but twice, I saw a flying beetle pass by as close as three feet to me. Boy, what an experience."

As he finished speaking a wide grin spread across his face as all of us picked up small stones and gently heaved them at him.

Dinner was a joint venture and we finally settled at the table to eat. Carlos was more animated than usual so naturally we let him speak first.

"This trapezoidal structure is more of a mystery than I first figured on." He quickly turned to me saying, "I need you on this Eric," then continued his story. "I have yet to find an entrance, if there even is one."

"What about the underground part of the temple ?" I asked.

Carlos gazed at me again with an almost disconcerted

expression.

"**I**'m not so sure now that there is anything underground. The thing really has me at a loss. Even its construction is something I have not come across before."

This statement caught us all off guard. Nothing has ever stumped Carlos before.

"Is it newer or older ?" quizzed Mario.

"**Y**es" was Carlos's answer with a smile. "I'm embarrassed to say I really don't know."

"**O**kay then." Mario asserted himself. "Tomorrow all five of us go and we'll figure this out."

No one objected, in fact it sounded like a good project with all five participating and working together.

" *This really is a great group,* " I thought.

Carlos was asked to further outline his thoughts but he deferred to Diego and me. I let Diego do the explaining, after all it was his theory and artistic eye that discerned this wonderful secret. We decided the disguised trees worked well considering four to five hundred years ago your average soldier was only thinking survival not artistic design.

After debriefing our entire day's outing we turned again to Carlos and Mateo. I for one was anxious for more detail.

"**T**he morning will be better suited for that Eric." explained Carlos. "It's getting late and it's quite obvious from your appearance you need some rest. We can go over more detail on the way there tomorrow," he followed with a compassionate smile.

I thanked him for his concern and agreed that some rest was very welcomed. We all cleaned up after dinner and I happily made my way to my hammock. As tired as I was, I was looking forward to sharing my day with Dove of Spring. Even if we did not connect mentally, just the thought of sharing with her as I did with my Maya friends I found emotionally satisfying. I could feel sleep taking over my body before I even lay down. I mentally fought this while reaching out to Violet. I faded from the conscience world with the words *"Good Night My Love"*

I woke up totally renewed to a beautiful clear blue sky. I suddenly realized the sun isn't usually up that high when I get up. Carlos, Mario and Mateo were chatting comfortably having already finished breakfast. They let Diego and I sleep on. The two of us arrived at the coffee pot together to the usual harassment for being lazy. The day ahead had already been planned and the necessary food and equipment already packed. It wasn't long before the five of us were on our way. The trail was relatively clear which made for easy hiking. As promised Carlos filled me in on what his thoughts were. It was going to be quite a day, the five of us searching for any indication to the purpose of this wonderful structure.

As we approached the outer wall I pointed out to Diego the false trees between the living. This appeared to fascinate him and he let the four of us go on while he studied this half living wall.

It was like discovering this temple for the first time; it had been so long since I was here last. A couple of years I believe. Without realizing it I distanced myself from the others and treated myself to a very close walk around the whole perimeter taking in every detail I could. At first I thought it was just my imagination yet I detected a very slight construction difference on the different sides. My curiosity piqued, I made a second walk around the massive, though not high piece of ancient architecture. Each side was unique to itself yet all fitted a preplanned length and height. There were no actual steps but the not too severe angle allowed a man to walk to the top, which of course I could not resist. The flat top I guessed to be about fifty feet per side. It truly was a massive platform. There was not much to view from the flat top surface because the jungle trees surrounding the temple still overshadowed the area. Perhaps hundreds of years ago there was something to see but for some reason I had my doubts. I don't think it was built as a viewing platform. The overall mystery of its function still begs to be solved by us, or at least Carlos.

I heard my name being called which broke my dream state. My four Maya friends were also now walking up to join me. They had been seeking me out for a while until Mateo happened to glance up.

I lay out my speculations of the four sides of different construction techniques. Carlos smiled when he heard my view point.

"Did I not say I needed you on this. I'm happy to say I was right."

Mario and Mateo were walking the outer perimeter of this massive flat top when Mario called for our attention. As we joined them

Mateo, not uttering a word, pointed down. There, a few inches from the edge, was a Glyph enclosed by a border of wavy lines. It was about fifteen inches in length and half that wide. It appeared weathered by the years but not worn by foot traffic.

"There is one of these centered on every side and each one different. Only one has a slight familiarity to me, the other three I had never seen before."

Naturally we all trekked to all four sides each giving his own judgement. The only consensus was that they were all different.

Leaving Mario and Mateo to further investigate the Glyph's, we three descended again to examine my theory of different construction.

Silently and slowly we navigated the outer wall, each making our own notes of what we considered different. Back at our starting point we compared opinions. Sure enough we listed many in congruencies. The type of stone, how it was cut, the fit together, and even the texture of the finished product was unlike the others. This was when we observed that only one side was fit to walk on. The others were actually dangerous. Diego volunteered to tell the others. We did not need any unnecessary accidents.

"Now to look into the reason behind this," Carlos muttered aloud.

"Could it be as simple as a competition," I suggested. "Think about the Glyph's on the platform. They could represent four different factions."

"That's as good a reason as any I suppose. It just seems so simple." replied Diego.

"You mean to tell me there was no simplicity with your ancients ?" I questioned with a smile.

"Could be," Carlos interjected also smiling. "Perhaps we are the ones who make everything complicated. Seriously though, why was this built ? Eric in your walk around did you notice anything that could be construed as an entrance ?"

"No, but come to think of it, I was so fascinated by the construction methods I wasn't looking for an entranceway."

"What do you say we walk the perimeter again, together

this time and play off each others sightings." Carlos proposed.

"Let's make this a five way search." Diego suggested.

All agreed and picked a corner point to start.

Before actually starting I took a compass sighting aligned with the wall edge and backed it up with GPS readings. I repeated this function at all four corners for further study back at camp at the map table.

Off we went looking for an entrance to the interior of this strange building. We took our time and circled it twice. There were three possibilities we all agreed on with none of them netting positive results. Discouraged somewhat we made ourselves comfortable on the ground with water and snacks. Mateo walked further away from the group to get an overall view of the setting. It was an impressive sight. There had to be an importance of some kind indicated by the wall construction around the entire area.

"Hey guys." he suddenly yelled, "Come have a look at this."

We begrudgingly arose from our resting place and joined Mateo. He pointed to the ground where we were now standing.

"Even after hundreds of years there is a definite shape on the ground," he stated.

He was right. It was difficult to pick out at first but with study a rectangular shape did show itself. It measured round about four feet by seven feet and aligned perpendicular to the center of the temple complex. Diego turned away to the right and started walking.

"Where are you going ?" we asked collectively.

"To check the other three sides of course.." He answered grinning.

Mario went with him The pair returned in twenty minutes.

"Same thing on all sides." was the report.

"If you ask me," I interrupted. "We have to dig. I know you said you don't believe this temple goes very deep underground, but to me this suggests a way to the center on this odd structure."

"Is this you talking or are you in touch with the king ?" inquired Mario.

"I'm afraid this is purely me this time. It's really only a

wild hunch."

Carlos joined with,

"Perhaps only a hunch but I concur. So let's dig."

No more was questioned as we all carefully chose a side and softly dug just outside the rectangle. Diego copied my earlier technique by probing slowly in the middle to see if he could detect anything solid. He was happily successful on his first try without going too deep. Our digging was then more enthusiastic. Soon before us was a wooden cover with strange markings. More of a design than letter markings. We stood back looking at each other, each awaiting a suggestion from the other for the next step.

Carlos moved to hands and knees looking for a handle or locking device. I joined him having done this many times in the desert.

"There you are," Carlos was heard to mumble.

Slowly, the center three foot by five foot section angled down about four feet allowing dirt and small stones to slide into the opening. Instinctively we all grabbed for our lanterns. The dirt neatly piled itself on a flat surface and once illuminated, led to steps downward.

My thoughts drifted north. *"This reminds me of my desert pyramid."*

Speaking of the desert, Dove of Spring materialized in my mind then left just as fast.

"Are you going down the steps or just stand there in the way ?." kidded Carlos.

"Oh, sorry. I drifted for a moment."

"She must be quite a woman!" He added.

"Does it show that much ?" I beamed.

Using my light to guide me I started down the steps.

"Be prepared to be amazed Eric."

"Here we go with the riddles."

"This will be extremely unusual for all of you."

"Can you give me a clue as to why ?"

I knew I would not receive an answer but I had to ask.

Getting back now to paying attention to what I'm presently doing, I found myself in a narrow corridor. Why I was the one going first I don't know but the other four were trailing behind me. I followed the passageway for an unmeasured distance, but I guesstimated we were close to the middle of the temple, and were at last facing a door of sorts. I willingly stepped aside to let Carlos work his magic fingers. The door was opened in short order but only showed another corridor, however this was more defined. The walls and overhead were polished smooth, even the floor was a finer texture. I was surprised, yet not, based on the king's recent words.

Carlos continued in the lead for a brief distance until faced with another sealed portal of a much fancier design. I assumed this was a foretelling of something inside. Anticipation filled the air as Carlos sought the opening mechanism.

The door slid noiselessly into the wall with no noticeable opening. Our lanterns gave their illumination freely bouncing off gold, silver, jewels and silks that adorned a throne like golden chair. We were obviously viewing the rear of this magnificent chair. One could tell the chair was occupied, by who we knew not. We fanned out in both directions circling the throne inching our way to the front. Torches adorned the walls every four feet which we lit as we passed. The chamber glowed as if filled by the sun. Then we were awe struck. The throne was occupied by a beautiful woman. A very beautiful woman. The bigger shock was that it was a white skinned woman. Nothing resembling Maya ancestry was visible. She was adorned in veils and silks you would expect to find in Egypt. Her entire personage reflected ancient Egypt. The king was correct. We were all speechless. The silence, only broken by the sizzle of flaming torches, seemed to go on forever.

What was this ? Was this a mummy ? Was it a carved statue, almost lifelike ? If it was a mummy, the mummification process was beyond words. The closest thing I could think of to describe it was the wax museum. Of course this was our first glimpse without investigation.

"What is this place ?" Carlos managed to whisper rhetorically.

"You did bring your camera." Mario stated directly to me as if it was an order.

"Yes, it's in my pack which of course is outside."

No one could take their eyes off this woman, who ever she was.   Each of us gradually worked themselves from the charm of this unknown woman. Donning our scientific persona's once more we sat about recording this magnificence.   I left to retrieve my camera and returned within six minutes.   I did not want to miss a thing.

On the way back with my camera my thoughts drifted to Whispering Wind and the world wide contracts he showed.

"Why not." I thought.   *"If the Navajo can have contact with Egypt then so can the Maya."*

"These connections go further than you think. Be patient and all will be revealed."

I expected a word from the king and I replied quickly, "I'll not answer you now. I'll leave that till later when I'm alone."

"As you wish Eric."

The king surprised me with his second remark, usually he tunes me out before I can answer.

Finally returning to the temple room it appeared as if my four Mayan colleagues had not moved. I can't say as I blame them. This was a ravishingly handsome woman. I imagine in real life she was even more so.

Before starting any conversations with the guys I immediately set about practicing my chosen profession. It was very difficult not to keep looking at the lady on the throne. I photographed this beauty from all angles. The scene before me was so stunning I almost could not stop clicking the shutter. This was almost too good to be true and I was thinking ahead. This was going to be next to impossible to convince the outside world.

I did at last get control of myself and proceed to shoot the rest of the room. The serious work finally over I turned my eyes to some self satisfaction, viewing closely, everything in the room. The silks reminded me of the material carefully hugging the book that was so dear to Whispering Wind. To all the Navejo for that matter.

There was a small bench directly across from the throne, empty of course, but the workmanship it contained was breathtaking. The woman occupying the golden chair was obviously well revered. The big question of course, who was she ?

The initial shock finally wearing off, whispering conversation began. We all agreed on Egypt but that was all any of us could come up with. The who, where, how and why of it remained a mystery.

I reiterated the story of the contracts the "Dineh" possessed and also brought up the mural hallway, where Egyptian sailing vessels were reproduced. My Maya friends, for once appeared to be at a total loss for an explanation. This connection was not part of any of their teachings or historical studies.

Diego was the first to approach the throne. You could see the artistic curiosity in his eyes. He studied the figure forever moving closer. We all watched as he dared touch the hand on the arm rest He quickly removed his hand while bringing his eyes closer. He tapped the hand with his fingernail, listening intently. He stood back, looking amazed and turned to the rest of us.

"The hand is gold, painted gold."

Astonished once more the four of us just stood there.

"I thought I detected a brush stroke which is why I wanted a closer look." Diego explained. "I was right and the mix of paint is a perfect flesh tone even down to the shadow imperfections. I honestly believe this is a pure gold statue created to lifelike perfection and then painted to represent reality. Look here." He instructed as he parted some of the silk material that made up the gown to expose a lifelike leg.

He tapped that also to show the hollow toned vibration.

Meaning no disrespect, we all drew nearer to listen as Diego repeated his tapping. The sound was definitely of a metallic source while at the same time a sort of muted sound.

Mario now moved closer and tapped it himself using a

coin. The sound was unlike any other metal sound. Mateo also joined Mario. They seemed to be thinking the same thing. Carlos nodded as if in the same thought wavelength. He went one step further by folding back some of the silk drapery exposing the upper leg. There was no flesh color, only pure gold. Normal skin wrinkles showed in detail. This was no ordinary mummification process or a gold sculpture. This was an actual human body covered in a layer of liquid gold. The exposed parts were then painted a true flesh color. This woman is real or was real, depending on how one wishes to view her presence here. Carlos commented, matter of fact, this process will require a more detailed study. This certainly was not any normal preservation technique. We mutually decided to do a thorough search of the throne room to see if we could find any other clues or hints of who this grand lady was or what her connection to the Maya was.

Each of us picked an object in the room and proceeded to examen it from all angles. Carlos had chosen an earthen jar, beautifully adorned with a tight fitting lid. He struggled with the lid, but did so carefully. Managing its secret the jar was opened.

"Looks like more scrolls for you to copy Eric," he said half laughing.

I joined him as he proceeded to unroll the cloth document.

"This is something new. I have never seen this format before."

I gazed at the scroll he was holding and was struck speechless.

"A contract !" I shouted. Then apologized for being so loud. "It's a contract. That's exactly the same thing I witnessed back with the Navajo. They were from peoples all over the world. It proved what no one wants to believe was possible."

I then pointed out all the detail as Whispering Wind had described to me including the signature made at the lower right corner. At least that's what Whispering Wind called it for lack of a better description. This particular mark was from Egypt. That much I was sure of.

"At least that fits with our golden lady's presence."

We were all so enthralled by this discovery we forgot our own chosen searches. Back to my own selected object, a small chest, more a miniature chest. It was beautifully constructed of highly polished dark wood with metal hinges, corners and hasp. There was no key hole but was locked just the same. I turned it every which way looking for some sort of trigger device to open. There was nothing that I could easily see, so I placed it back on the floor in its corner. As I did so the lid slowly swung open. This fascinated me to the point I just could not resist. I closed the cover again and heard a faint click locking it. Sure enough I could not open it. Feeling defeated by a simple box I set it down once again. Much to my surprise the lid swung open. Not daring to touch it I moved my eyes closer to peek inside. What I saw took me by surprise. A poorly woven cloth from a rough and dirty yarn of sorts presented itself. The unsubtle folds showed it secreted something. I did not hesitate to withdraw this old bundle from the box.

"**O**dd," I thought. "A chest of the highest quality workmanship and material hiding a dirty old cloth. To me that was like wearing your old greasy jeans to get into your immaculate brand new Cadillac."

Now I'm being silly. I felt an odd sensation as I held it in my hand as if I was prying into some one's personal secret. For what ever reason it led me to think of Dove of Spring. A very private person whom I wanted to know better. The words of Whispering Wind repeated themselves in my mind.

*"**S**he will be of great assistance to you in the future. Do not let that escape you."*

"**A**re you going to open that or just hold it forever thinking of her."

Mario's words broke my trance like state. Feeling myself blush I stumbled for an answer. He was smiling as I looked up at him.

"**I** found nothing but noticed this beautiful box you were playing with"

He picked it up from the floor and the top closed with the same click I heard earlier. With a serious expression I asked him to please open it again. He tried as I had earlier and then looked at me. I was now smiling.

"**J**ust put it back on the floor," I said quietly.

He did as I asked and watched, amazed as I was, as the lid swung open. We both grinned as I explained.

"**I** don't know why or how either, It just did."

"**W**e'll look at that later, open the rag."

"**A**s good a name as any for it," I answered.

I peeled back the cloth only to reveal a chunk of turquoise. The bluest and purist either of us had ever seen. Its size filled my hand completely and must have weighed four or five pounds. We stared in awe.

"**T**his is getting weird now," I mumbled.

"**A**nother connection of the Navajo and Maya and now Egypt." Mario stated, then called the others to look.

"**T**his is getting weird now," Carlos exclaimed using my exact words.

Mario and I laughed to the confusion on Carlos' face.

"**D**id I say something funny ?" he asked.

Mario explained what we laughed at. I then proceeded to explain the mysterious box. Carlos knew right away. He had seen this type before. One of the legs of the chest was actually the opening mechanism.

Now that the easy mystery was cleared up all we had left was, who was she and why was she here.

Nothing else presented itself in the way of clues or identity of our golden lady. I photographed the scroll before returning it to its resting place. Diego also took a Polaroid of the paper for us to continue studying back at camp.

We all slowly wandered back to the throne. The magnetic appeal of the woman was disturbing and unlike the king we could not converse.

Again the king's message came to mind. *"These connections go further than you think, Be patient and all will be revealed."* I hoped the king would be receptive tonight, then perhaps we can get some insight to the presence of Egypt in the Yucatan.

As Carlos was attempting to return the scroll to the jar he had trouble getting it in. Realizing something was blocking the easy access he reached down with his free hand into the opening then suddenly a smile crossed his lips. There was another scroll. Actually not a scroll he realized as he withdrew his hand. He was clasping what looked like a bunch of rags bundled or rolled up together. We all crowded around Carlos as he slowly peeled apart the strange bundle. There were eleven individual bits of cloth each approximately twelve by twelve inches in size, though not exact. They all had wavy lines drawn helter scelter on the material. This fabric Mateo identified as very thin, well tanned camel hide.

The wavy lines were both solid and broken along with dots scattered here and there, next to the lines and away from them.

"Pieces of maps," I said my thoughts aloud.

Suddenly all eyes were on me, skeptically. I almost had not realized I spoke out loud.

"Oh, sorry guys. These drawings just reminded me of the maps I saw along with the Navajo treasures and contracts and also what we ourselves found at the kings tomb.

Enlightenment took hold and recognition followed. Soon all were on board with my description. We spread out the pieces like a jig saw puzzle and started matching areas. We were pretty certain we identified the Mediterranean Sea starting out from Egypt. Another was definitely the west coast of Africa.. Again another section was the southern tip of North America continuing down through Central America and on to the coast line of South America. On a separate cloth was, without a doubt, the Carribean and Gulf of Mexico with numerous markings around the Yucatan.

Carlos was able to identify the China sea and the isles of Japan. The last four pieces were parts of the west coast of North America right up through Alaska.

With our puzzle complete we stood there dumbfounded. No one would believe this impossibility. Here we are thinking we were an advanced culture. We're still working on making maps yet here we are looking at navigational aids from who knows how many thousands of years ago.

This ties in well with all the contracts found with my desert friends treasures. There was obvious world wide contact and trade long before current historians will admit to.

This must have been what the king was referring to by his words; *"These connections go further than you think."* I definitely must talk with him tonight.

Mario, again being practical alerted us.

"I hate to break up this fun party guys but it will be dark

soon. If we want to get back to camp before that happens we should seriously consider heading back very soon."

No one really wanted to leave but common sense finally won out. All agreed, a second or even third visit would be essential to our serious studies.

Thanks to Mario's alertness we made it back to camp just in time, in fact the last hundred yards or so were a bit tricky in the dark. Thank goodness we did have a few lanterns with us. We all turned to for dinner of sorts. We just ate whatever we could manage with out fussing.

Carlos began our debriefing with an obvious statement.

"About the only thing we learned today was there was an emissary from Egypt who stayed a while with our ancestors. Her real mission and how she arrived here is still a mystery as is her being mummified with gold. I for one am glad the Spanish did not discover her tomb."

Both Mario and Mateo could not recall any such process of body painting with gold in any of their past studies.

"Perhaps this is something they brought with them from Egypt. She could not have come here alone yet there is no other signs of her countrymen," suggested Mateo.

"None that we found yet," I added. "I still say we have a lot more searching to do in and around that complex. Remember, Mario and Diego checked the other three sides and reported similar rectangles there also. We must research and dig there. Who knows what else they may lead to. I know I'm going right back to my aerial photography, just not tonight, I'm much too tired."

The group conferred for another hour coming up with absolutely nothing new. Our day's efforts finally caught up with us all and a good nights rest was our answer to a busy day. I personally was very happy the evening ended. I wanted to talk with the king.

Comfy in my hammock and tuned into my jungle music interlude I set my thoughts to the king. Luck was with me. In less than a minute I received my answer.

"I am here as you desired my young friend.

What is it you wish ?"

"**A**n answer to the mysterious lady of gold. You said the connection goes farther than you think. That sounds good but what is the connection and what is to be revealed ?"

"You're impatience surprises me Eric. You are customarily so calm and resigned. Again you need not my help. Review all that is before you and you shall have your answer."

The fading out of the words was an answer I was most familiar with. The king as usual left me hanging. I expected it but that didn't make it any easier on my difficulty. Perhaps he is right though, maybe I'm not thinking deep enough.

Eric readily dismissed the king and turned his thoughts to Violet. He closed his eyes and drifted to her on the music of the surrounding jungle.

Chapter 12

Eric awoke to the chattering tree top monkeys although his thoughts of the kings last words immediately filled his head.

"Review all that is before you."

"That's easy for him to say, he already knows the answer. That's no way to start your day Eric. Calm yourself and try to think logically."

Self chastisement worked and Eric wished Dove of Spring a good morning as he went straight for the coffee pot. Diego was already there and the coffee all prepared. It wasn't long before the others joined them. Of course the conversation instantly turned to our "Golden Lady". Trying to be the stability of the group, Carlos put forth a plan for the day which did not include visiting our Egyptian guest. We all knew he was correct, and that we all do the work we came for. I would be the only one free to return to the unique parallelogram since I was sort of a freelance person. This of course thrilled me but I chose to stay with the group knowing I could be of assistance some place. If not I would return to my air photo work and the tunnel entrance. It also gave me more time to follow the kings advice and *"Review all that is before you and you shall have your answer."* There were so many ultra interesting things to do it could stagger one's mind if allowed.

I chose to stay in camp and be chief cook and bottle washer for the day. After being bored all day in the jungle I figured it would be nice for them to return to meals all ready prepared so they could just relax.

Actually, truth be told, I was in a rather lazy mood today.

Perhaps lazy is the wrong operative word, confused is more like it. I just could not make a sound decision as to what to occupy my time with. I refilled my mug and opened my journal and as soon as I did, Dove of Spring jumped off the page. I didn't mean to purposely waste time but she occupied my thoughts for almost a quarter of an hour. I guess I m committed now. Funny, I did not find that idea so awful either. I smiled and started writing in my journal about the Golden Lady.

I think I captured everything in the throne room with her, at least to the best of my right now memory. I also knew the others would be updating their journals with the same information. I'm sure between the five of us we will not leave anything slip by. I paused a moment thinking about the lady on the throne. Everything about her appeared to fit the Egyptian theme from head to toe. I was in the act of closing the journal when another flash went off in my head. Never mind my head, the Golden Lady's head is what came to mind. The head piece she was wearing. Now that I think of it, it almost did not fit with the rest of her attire. I just could not put my finger on what or why. I'm surprised none of the others picked up on it either. I believe the gold painted body is what captured everyone's attention. I would definitely bring this to the attention of the others.

The temptation was great and it was a struggle to keep myself in camp but common sense prevailed and I remained.

As usual I was the only one who did not hear the lunch bell go off. The guys wandered in as they always did. I was however prepared. Chatter was light and lunch quick. I promised a big dinner so they could all relax.

Promising the big dinner was a bit premature when I realized I had nothing special. As I indicated earlier I was in a lazy mood and work of any kind did not really appeal to me, but suddenly fishing did.

I was very successful thanks to my teachers. Their techniques to this jungle fishing paid off nicely. I brought back eleven good sized I don't know what you call them. But they were very tasty.

I was able to serve an interesting meal. Fish served in a fruit mixture I experimented with. It turned out better than I expected if I do say so myself. I added some jungle green salad again with some fruit juice dressing on the side. All we were lacking was the wine. Water and or coffee would have to do.

Like clockwork the crew drifted back to camp looking a bit bedraggled but at least smiling when they saw the fish.

When I felt their appetite had been satisfied and they were relaxed it was only then I broached the subject of the Golden Lady. In a purposely round about way I tried to get their views on the lady's headgear. For the most part I drew blank expressions, which is what I expected. With a silly grin they admitted not too much attention was paid except for the fact that she was quite beautiful.

"Exactly," I exclaimed. "Then it hit me this morning. I kept seeing something different, but I didn't know what. I could not identify anything.   Finally, this afternoon I recalled a picture of the statue of Nefertiti. For now that's where I'm going to leave it until we can get back there, all of us, to further investigate what I'm thinking."

Mario, beaming a silly grin, commented,

"You've been hanging around the king too much, now you're talking in riddles."

Of course this brought laughter from everyone. They enjoyed me being the brunt of their clowning. I couldn't help but laugh with them. Who knows, perhaps I am starting to think in riddles. *Perish the thought"*

I told them I would let them take the lead on the return visit. I did not want to interfere with their preplanned work schedule any more than I already had.

"You mean we have to go back to the boring paper work again," complained Diego laughing.

"As I said, I don't want to interfere," I replied.

"That may be true, but look what your interference has netted us already," commented a very serious Carlos. "Okay, you win. Tomorrow we go back to the "Golden Lady".

This actually made everyone happy. Especially me.

~ ~ ~ ~ ~ ~

Without even thinking about it we all rushed through breakfast anxious to view the special lady once more.

We made good time getting there but still dallied outside

before entering. Viewing this engineering feat never grows old.

Not wanting to push my excitement I let the group have whatever time they deemed necessary to admire this unique organization of stone. . I must admit it was totally different than anything else any of us came across to date.

Slowly, as if on purpose, which I knew was not the case, we all drifted to the special portal entrance down to the center of the partial pyramid structure. I could feel my heart pounding with excitement. I obviously have gotten myself worked up far too much. *"What if my thoughts don't pan out."* I thought. *"What a let down."* I then thought of how I would have wasted another day of the teams time, taking them away from real research just to follow my own pipe dream. *"Keep your fingers crossed Eric."*

Once we were all present in the throne room, Carlos spoke up.

"Okay, Eric. You can explain your riddle now."

He did say it with a smile, it was not an order.

Reciprocating the smile, I then turned to Diego.

"Go ahead Diego. Since you were the one to discover the gold covering, Let's see what you can determine about the headdress."

Now I actually did cross my fingers.

Diego hesitantly approached our "Golden Lady" and ever so gently tapped his finger just above the forehead at the start of the head piece. His eyes tightened as if in thought, he moved his finger higher up the outer covering and tapped again. There was the same sound. His curiosity showing he looked at me for approval. I nodded okay. Carefully and with reverence he began to remove the head covering. To the surprise of all this was not an oval or oblong hat. This shaped head covering was made specially to fit the "Golden Lady's" head.

Open mouthed we all gaped at the elongated skull. This was not an uncommon practice of the Maya of old or those of Noble birth anyway. Just after birth the head is wrapped with cloth and hardened board to force the elongated growth of the head to eventually take the shape of the head of a serpent. This was done for religious purposes as much as nobility identification.

Mario then voiced what everyone was thinking.

"**T**his is what you had in mind when you riddled about Nefertiti."

I shook my head yes along with a broad smile,

"**I**'m just hypothesizing but there is an off chance she could be related to her. It has been written by some that Nefertiti did have a hint of Maya appearance."

Carlos picked up from there in a more serious tone.

"**S**he could have been Mayan all along and now returned."

The room went silent.

Mateo, almost in a whisper added,

"**P**ossibly an offspring of Nefertiti, sent here as an emissary."

Silence again returned to the room.

Carlos, the ever practical one, brought the discussion back to actual known facts.

"**L**et's face it, first, no one is ever going to believe us, even with the :Golden Lady" here as proof. Second, no one is ever going to believe the Maya - Egyptian connection. Laughingly he mumbled, "There are those scholars of today who still believe Columbus discovered America." Pausing a bit he went on, "Think of how many true professionals do you know who are going to get to come here to view all we have uncovered.   There are those who won't even travel to view finds or anomalies found in the States never mind coming down to travel three days into the jungle. And in the states we are only talking about a few hours driving distance."

We were all surprised with his negativism. This was not like Carlos at all.

"**S**orry guys." he apologized. "I didn't mean to put a damper on the discovery. Okay, where do we go from here ?" He now put on an apologetic smile.

Feeling his frustration I comforted with, "I agree with your feeling one hundred percent. About the only thing that will be accepted by the scholars is the actual city and the area it covers. Though I don't think the Department of Antiquities will have a problem accepting what's in the throne room."

The air lightened somewhat with my statement.

"As far as where do we go from here, we can discuss that at length later. Right now I want to photographically document this. Especially the face. Let's see if there is a match to Nefertiti"

While I plied my trade, with Diego's help, the others did a more detailed search of the throne room

"Look here guys." Mateo called with the thrill of a child in his voice. He had found a closed panel under the bench and from it now held a toy replica of an Egyptian sailing ship. Toy may be the wrong word, let's just say a miniature scale model. They were passing it around like children do. Diego held it still long enough for me to get a few camera shots. I must admit the workmanship was exquisite. Diego took some Polaroid shots so he could compare it with the ship in the mural hallway. We agreed to leave the ship where we found it lest it be accidently damaged.

What else was to be done here. My curiosity and hunch were satisfied. We thoroughly fine toothed combed every square foot of the room and its furnishings for a second time. Nothing new made its presence known.

Mario, Diego and myself headed back to camp while Carlos and Mateo stayed to give the outside and the surrounding area another search, particularly the other three sides and what could be other entrances to who knows where or what.

Upon arrival at camp I quickly set about storing away the film for safety sake. These undeveloped negatives were much too valuable to just be left around subject to the heat and moisture of the jungle. Satisfied that they were as good as I can do here without refrigeration, I joined Mario and Diego at the table with my mug of coffee. What we just went through was not physically demanding but that's the way I felt. I guess it was the emotional excitement. I drank deeply of the thick black liquid and sighed with relief.

"Boy ! It's so good to sit down," I cried.

"I can see your thinking trend with this Golden Lady, but there is an awful lot to consider before we make any brash statements we may be sorry for later," Mario put forth.

"I couldn't agree more with what you are saying," I replied. "We definitely need more input from the king on this,"

Diego posed.

"*Yes, but will we get it.*" This thought ran through my head. "We should wait for Carlos and Mateo before we open any serious discussions." I suggested.

"Let's see what we can dig up for dinner." Diego said, already looking through the supplies. "You know Eric, you have all of us spoiled."

"How did you come up with that idea ?" I questioned.

"Well, with all that's been happening it just seems like this would be a great Cognac night," he smiled.

Mario added with an even bigger smile, "I'll have to agree with that."

"Okay, I'll run right down to the local liquor store. Hold dinner for me."

Carlos and Mateo returned just before dinner. They did locate another potential entry on the opposite face of the pyramid. But without the proper tools and short on time, further investigation would have to wait.

We all knew we had a lot to discuss. Even Carlos brought up the fact of the possibility the king could enlighten us on what we were facing. I was the first to agree with that but also cautioned of his customary lack of total cooperation in such things. I brought up his last words to me; **"Review all that is before you and you shall have your answer."**

With smiles they all answered with about the same words, "Well, that helps a whole lot."

"Now you see what I'm up against sometimes, with his riddles"

"It's amazing you got anything out of him," commented Mateo.

"Okay now," Mario took over. "Let's lay out what we do have as definite and then we can all add our suppositions and see if that nets us anything."

We all turned in our thoughts and Mario recorded them on paper while we ate. Believe it or not we had quite a list.

"Now for the fun part," smiled Mario grabbing another piece of paper.

"Okay, let's just go around the table. We'll start with you Eric, since you started this whole thing."

I accepted the jest in the way it was meant.

After listing the obvious from all of us, now the hard part, the what and whys. The best we could do were guesses, some educated, some not so much. The biggest monkey wrench in the mess came from Mateo.

"If I'm not mistaken in my memory from some of my past readings, Nefertiti was the wife of Amenhatep IV."

"Okay, so what does that have to do with this ?" questioned Carlos, showing a little impatience.

"Well...." Mateo replied with a slight smile. "He ruled about fourteen forty eight or there about's." Here he paused then added. "B.C."

Diego to keep the mood light said quietly,

"Which came first, the chicken or the egg ?"

There was a slight hesitation before we all broke out on a laugh. His words served their purpose. We weren't here to argue but to seriously discuss.

Carlos then joined again. "That does pose a good question. Did they travel to us or we to them ? Did we start the practice of scull flattening, or did they ? Did we build the first pyramids or did they ?

Just imagine how much more information we would have if the missionary explorers had not destroyed and burned our ancient books and writings only because they feared them. Talk about ignorance."

This remark had a sobering effect on everyone.

"Based on what Eric mentioned earlier, the Navejo also had contact with the Egyptians."

"When that was has not been determined yet." I threw in.

Carlos indicated a thank you with a head nod and continued.

"So all we really know for sure is that we have an Egyptian lady buried here in the Yucatan. And let's face it, no one is even going to believe that. As impossible as this seems we know it's real because we see it and are living it."

He said this, this time without bitterness.

Mateo wisely posed. "The fact is, this dilemma is going to take more than just the five of us to figure out, never mind solve."

Then looking directly at me with a big smile said,

"See the mess you got us into ? You and your discoveries."

"Okay." I answered, "I'll make that two bottles of Cognac each."

Every one was happy again.

We ended our night with a general conversation about nothing and mutually decided it was a long day and rest was needed. I truly favored this idea, I wanted to get in touch with Dove of Spring and the king, not necessarily in that order. As I zipped up the netting and lay back I never realized how welcoming a simple hammock could be.

~ ~ ~ ~

Getting in touch with Violet, though briefly it was, was easier than I thought. I assumed it was because of her desire to hear from me. Whatever the reason I welcomed it. Her message, though short and sweet, was given with a sincerity that was growing in both of us.

Return to me, I will always be here for you.

I knew then I was totally committed to this woman.

Now if only it was that easy to reach the king. I tried my best for close to an hour with no results. I some times wonder if it is not that way on purpose. Oh well, my music is calling.

Chapter   13

I was awake before my screeching treetop friends. Jokingly I thought of locating their sleeping spots and blasting off an air horn just to see their reaction. *"Knock it off Eric, you're getting carried away again."* I laughed to myself.

Even though it was early I felt great. I don't remember awakening at all last night. I happily, but quietly, made my way to the coffee pot, preparing the mornings elixir. I wondered what the day would bring.

Once the black brew was finished I filled my mug and slowly headed in the direction of the tomb. No particular reason and was just meandering and enjoying the environs without a care in the world.

"This is the way I prefer to see you Eric. Do not let your mind questions cloud your sense of judgement."

"You mean being upset by not being able to solve your riddle ?" I laughed in response. "I must admit I do get frustrated now and then."

"I mean not to frustrate you my friend. You have an analytical mind and usually do not need my help. You have done well to date. What is it you need from me now ? Is it our Egyptian visitor that has you intrigued ?"

"That's about it." I replied. "Why the visit this far from home ? Why the tomb ? Why the gold body covering ? What is the connection ?"

"You and your friends have previously outlined the connection. As with the Navajo there was trade contact. Whispering Wind can further explain. You are correct in her connection to Nefertiti. When she arrived the head shape did not go unnoticed. She was welcomed as a Goddess returning from where the sun rises. There are legends of the chosen people leaving to the world of the East. For unknown reasons her life left her while here. She was entombed and preserved as befitting her station in life. The gold was chosen because it does not decay or diminish its glow. It will always be, therefore this royal personage will always be. The hidden tomb for obvious reasons. To safeguard their heritage from the greed of the slaughtering Europeans. Does that satisfy your ever curious mind."

Showing a slight discomfort by the kings address, Eric answered quietly that he was satisfied for now.
"But, I do have one more inquiry."

"I know the question still in your mind and of your Mayan friends. That I will not go into. History still has a lot to reveal if allowed. When the time is deemed right you will have your answer. Remember, as you already know the truth is not always accepted, particularly when it goes against wrongly established protocols."

"But how will we know when that time is ?"
My own words were echoing in my head. I was familiar with the signal. I was alone once again with just my coffee.

I wandered a bit more digesting the kings words. As usual, when you break them down they always fall into place to show logic and how, to accept and use them. I noticed some movement back by the coffee pot and walked in that direction. Mateo extended his morning greeting commenting on my early rise.

"At least it payed off," I smiled. "The king and I had a nice chat which of course I will share with everyone at breakfast."

"Sounds ominous," answered a serious Mateo.

"On the contrary. It answered a lot of our questions. Not all, but most."

One by one the other three joined us with coffee. We talked about getting breakfast but I could see how anxious everyone was to hear of the kings words. I refilled my mug and started my replay of my conversation with Atl. I repeated almost word for word how he answered my query. I especially emphasized his answer to my unasked question.

The five of us now silent as we thought and sipped. Mario was the first to move from the table.

"Okay, let's see what we can dig up for breakfast." All of us came out of our trance like mode and joined the world again. We further discussed yesterdays find and the kings enlightenment. Believe it or not it was an upbeat and logical discourse. It was decided and approved by all that we would go back to our normal routine and continue our normal research work on the city and its surrounding environs. At least that was something we knew would be accepted by the Archeological community. Something that could be added to history of the world. Our decision would be for the present anyway, we would not pursue anything further with our "Golden Lady". I don't know how the others felt but I was actually relieved. The pressure was off for now.

After breakfast Carlos, Mario and Mateo left to continue the paper work validation. Diego would do the same but first he wanted to do his comparison of the toy ship with the image in the wall mural. I was to join him after I finished my KP duty.

Clean up was easy and I was on my way to meet with Diego. I brought my camera along just from habit. I too was looking forward to seeing the comparison, though I expected it to be a perfect match. I don't know why, just a hunch. I really wouldn't expect anything less.

Diego was more than happy to see me, so he could share his excitement. The wall mural being so large the model would probably match in size. The Polaroid shots he took were more than adequate to see and compare. Every detail could be seen in the two as if they were one and the same, right down to both sails and oars. Diego was anxious to go back and bring the model here for a more detailed inspection, but better judgement won out. He knew it was not as important as the regular research work that was still to be done. He did say though that before the season ended he would make that match up.

Diego left to resume his boring paper work. I decided to go back to my aerial photography, who knows what else may show itself. While sorting through the photos I was mentally planning a return to the tunnel entrance to further explore and find the actual entrance way. I couldn't believe how excited I was becoming again at the thought of finding the portal. I also felt sure the others would not object to me going alone. The path was well marked now and known to all.

Knowing that was to be my plan for tomorrow I set to work seriously looking at the photos. Gazing at the large map table of the total city layout I realized a section to the southwest I had not paid much attention to. Content with myself I set about finding the aerial coverage for that section. I was at home once more doing what I love to do.

Voices broke my concentration till I became aware that it must be lunch break again. I will have to get myself one of those internal alarm clocks my Mayan friends use. It worked out well though, my eyes could use the break. Lunch chatter was light mostly aimed at me for resting all day making believe I was working with my head resting on my stereo glasses.

"Just for that." I answered, "I may take back one of those bottles of Cognac."

That's when they accused me of getting nasty. All at once they headed back into the green canopy saying I could go back to sleep now. Back to the map table I did go, but not to sleep. Another few hours of concentration finally lead me to something. There was a small break in the jungle canopy. I could not detect any actual structures but I did read shadowing. Shadows that ran in straight lines. Small and not very lengthy but shadows none the less. Organized shadows I thought. I went back and forth between the high and low altitudes which were flown on different years but even that came up with the same shadow configuration.

"This definitely needs to be checked out," I said aloud.

"Do you always talk to yourself ?" Carlos inquired.

His voice sort of startled me but only for a second or two.

"What happened, did you get lost and could only find your way back here." I asked with a smile.

"I just wanted to check on you to make sure you weren't sleeping. It was my day to watch you," he quipped in return.

We laughed together before he added,

"I finished up the area I was checking and it is too late to get to the next area so I decided to come back and do some journal work. You seem involved, find something new ?"

"Perhaps, and not too far from here, just in the opposite direction from our other finds. Ground truthing will be the next step. I plan on returning to the tunnel entrance to confirm once and for all the above ground entrance and get it successfully plotted on the map."

"Are you planning on going alone ?"

"I thought I would. I didn't want to interfere with any of your recording work."

"And we appreciate that, but would you mind if I joined you tomorrow ?"

"Of course not, I think that would be great. You and I have not had a chance to chat freely. You will be most welcome."

"Thanks for that, it will give my head a rest from all this paper work."

Carlos then went to his journal work while I scrapped up the makings for dinner. Tonight appeared as if it would be a good night for all to relax and just enjoy life here in the jungle.

The rest of the day was routine for all. The other three returned in their normal manner and we enjoyed a casual dinner with the usual joking.

My guesswork about the night being one of relaxation proved correct, though not physically taxing, hour after hour of monotonous paper work can be very taxing to the mind. Relaxation is then a must in order to keep one's mind sharp.

   Both Carlos and I retired early. I took advantage of the time trying to commune with Dove of Spring, but it was not to be on this evening. However my mind drifted to the desert and life with Violet. I didn't expect it but I was not frightened by the idea. This pleased me as my serenade lulled me to sleep.

Chapter 14

Carlos was up early and had taken on the chore of coffee maker. This left me free to just relax and enjoy. We discussed basic plans for the day, eager to find the tunnel entrance. We both agreed it would most likely be filled with debris to naturally deter any one who accidently discovered it.

We both had a hearty breakfast and prepared some easy food for the journey there and back. We equipped ourselves with the usual, machete, digging tools, knives, GPS and camera. To top it off we slung our hammocks over the back packs knowing it would be at least one overnighter.

We left camp just before nine. We followed my plotted map that Diego and I had put together and sure enough we soon came upon the hidden air vent. Carlos wanted a closer look see so we dallied there for a short while he studied it from an engineering aspect. He also was fascinated by the false trees.

He made his feelings known with a mumbled comment,

"And they called these people primitive."

Satisfied with our discovery explanation, he also agreed that this was definitely an air vent to the underground.

We continued on our way following my GPS plot.

Carlos keen eyes also picked out a few more possible tree formations for air vents. This would have to be further researched at another time.

Surprisingly our jungle trek was not as bad as expected.

The jungle undergrowth yielded to our machete's quite easily though we both knew we still had a long journey ahead of us.

We had previously alerted the others it would most likely require a few days before our return because of the distances yet to be traveled.

We set a good pace and traversed a good distance despite the jungles interference now and then. Our luck stayed with us, for as it grew dark we came upon a natural cover of trees, ideal for an encampment and a place to hang our hammocks. We made only a small fire, just enough to heat our MRE's and turned in early. The days hike took its toll on our bodies.

I reviewed my day with Violet, then just let the jungle take me to dreamland.

~ ~ ~ ~

A restful night, a quick breakfast and we were again on our way in heightened anxiety. Early afternoon found us at the end of my map plotting, each of us trying to hide our excitement. Silence was the order for both of us as we scanned with our eyes. I followed my GPS to the second of the reading I had recorded while in the tunnel. I looked around, disappointed. I was not able to discern anything outstanding. It appeared that the whole jungle was one and the same. I switched off the GPS returning it to its case experiencing further disappointment I don't usually feel sorry for myself, but I started to.

"This is not like you Eric. You forget you have others to help you."

I then heard the all too familiar echo. Looking to Carlos I knew the king's message was for me alone. Carlos returned my gaze and smiled.

"Looks like you did it again my friend."

Confusion must have shown in my eyes. He continued with,

"You're standing in the middle of it I would guess."

I must have still looked bewildered. Laughing gently Carlos went on,

"Look around you. You're standing in a circle of trees. Yes jumbled undergrowth, but not trees. It's almost a perfect circle."

Feeling suddenly stupid I physically surveyed three hundred sixty degrees around where I was standing. Now I was also smiling. Carlos ignored my slight embarrassment and moved towards me suggesting we try and pinpoint something, anything that may lead to the tunnel entrance. Picking up on his cue I found a sizable stick and proceeded to tap all the trees surrounding the circle. It was now Carlos's turn to look befuddled. I explained this was Diego's technique of determining hollow trees.. A smile of recognition lit up his face. It grew even bigger when I produced a hollow sound.

While I continued my tree thumping Carlos started to dig in the middle of the circle. It was not long before our suspicions were satisfied. About three feet deep, buried debris showed itself. A few more test holes confirmed his first discovery.

I finished my tree search resulting in only two hollow trunks, actually quite close to each other. We both gave this some thought until Carlos suggested I try one more tree that was outside the circle. It was located close to the two chosen trees but spaced to form a triangle. His suspicions confirmed that it too was hollow.

With a huge grin he bid me to grab my digging tool and join him as he started to dig at the center of the triangle.

Between grunts and groans I asked,

"Why are we digging here ?"

"It just seemed logical to me at the time," Carlos answered. "A larger entrance would become obvious, hence the debris. So why not still have a smaller access way to the tunnel ?"

"But Diego and I checked the wall at the end."

"But did you go to the very end or just stop at the debris pile ?"

Feeling chagrined I admitted we stopped at the large entrance.

"Chances are the ancestors had all this figured ahead of time."

We halted our digging for a moment both now smiling. His logic appeared correct.

"So let's keep digging," Carlos smiled.

Another five minutes of serious shovel action discouragingly netted the start of unexpected debris. Carlos however was not in the least discouraged. It was almost as if he had a renewed energy.

"Don't stop now," he directed me. "We're almost there."

How he knew this I'll never know He obviously has a hidden knowledge of ancient structures. I'll not question anything that can help rescue hidden history.

After another fifteen minutes of digging and the moving of ancient debris we hit the jackpot. A rock slab shaped like a perfect rectangle but with rounded corners was staring up at us. I could feel my heart pounding as my eyes covered every square inch. I turned to Carlos who appeared to be in deep concentration. I chose not to disturb him and returned my attention to the chunk of rock before us. This was not just a slab of stone found lying around. This was obviously a work of art made specifically for this purpose. I sat down on the edge of our exposed hole studying the magnificent shaped rock. How do we lift such a weight with out modern tools. This thought brought to mind Lone Buffalo and his back hoe. If he only were here.

I moved deeper into the hole to feel around the edge of the obstacle now keeping us from the tunnel. In doing so some small loose rocks slid down the sides and bounced off the horizontal slab.

"Do that again," Carlos said quietly

I gazed up at him questioning.

"Do that again," he repeated. "Slide or drop some small stones on to the slab."

I did as he asked thinking he too may have gone over the edge like the rest of us. As I did so I realized what he was after. The sound was not stone on stone. It was more like stone on something hollow. Before I knew it Carlos was down in the hole beside me, pocket knife in hand. He immediately started scratching on the slab. Again the technology of the ancients showed its face. This wasn't a real stone. It was the same artificial composition as the false trees at the air vents stations. With a little hand digging we were able to lift the now not so heavy slab exposing stone steps.

Carlos was sporting a huge smile as he said.

"And you say there are tunnels through out North and South America like this ?"

With an equal happy grin I returned,

"I didn't say it. I'm just repeating others opinions from things that I have read."

"If this is really true though, one could make a career out of these searches."

"Yeah, and imagine how much history would be uncovered."

The make believe door opened rather easily, considering it had not been used for over four hundred years. With serious excitement we descended the steps only to find a wall not allowing further progress.

"This, I'm sure was just another safety precaution to discourage the fortune seekers," Carlos stated.

I shook my head in agreement as he set his magic fingers to work. In short order the familiar sounds of sliding stone filled the air. There was our tunnel.

It was a bit anticlimactic. We knew it was here, it just was just a matter of locating it. Well, we did, so now what ?

We entered the tunnel eight or ten feet or so. I felt better with an actual visual confirmation. Sure enough there was the cave in that injured Diego. Satisfied with my validation we returned above ground.

I documented the exact location with the GPS and so marked it on our working maps. As usual though it would not be exposed to the public eye until we finished our research of the entire city. We did not want looters and fortune seekers disturbing our historical findings.

We closed up the tunnel and disguised the entrance way as best we could, not really expecting visitors but you never know.

We chose to return to camp the way we came in order to give Carlos another chance to study the air vent system. Off we went satisfied at having solved another piece of our ever growing puzzle.

Our journey back to camp was routine. We had already blazed the trail so walking was not tedious at all. We stopped three times to look at air vents to the underground. Carlos's keen eyes identified two other locations. Based on what he learned at the one location we did some minor research.

        We dallied slightly longer at the first one he studied. You could tell he was making a lot of mental notes. Knowing how his mind works I'm sure he will have answers. When he appeared satisfied from his studies, in the workings of his own mind at least, we continued our trek back to home base. We had much to share again with our three comrades.

        Supper was ready and waiting and we did not hesitate to partake. It was the perfect opportunity to tell all of our days' success.

        Overall it was another pleasant evening as everybody turned to their own journals for updates.

        I was tired physically from the digging but mentally relaxed because of the successful results. Now alone in my hammock I again shared my day with Dove of Spring and allowed the sounds of the jungle ease me into undisturbed sleep.

Chapter 15

As planned the night before my four friends would return to the land of boredom and paper work while I would do a preliminary check on my suspicions surrounding items of interest found on the photos.

I left camp, with high hopes, just before eight o"clock, as did the others. They went their own separate ways to continue their boring paper work. I was headed to check out an anomaly I picked up on the air photos. It was the area to the South West of the tomb, which to date we had not thoroughly checked out. Actually we had not ever stretched out our searches in that direction at all. No matter how long I viewed the pictures of this particular area it still had me stumped.

As much as I enjoyed the company of my four Mayan friends there was something about being alone in the jungle that excited the very core of me; something that one cannot put a name to.

I promised not to go too far. Luckily the area of photo incongruity was only about two miles from the pyramid tomb.

Fortunately for me I did not have to do too much machete slashing. In fact there were areas I came across that almost looked as if they were used as trails. Not hard worn but cleared by frequent use.

"Don't be silly," I scolded myself "No one treaded these jungles in hundreds of years although drug cartel people did cross my mind for a second or two, but they're here for specific reasons, not to live.

At last my GPS notified me I was in the general area, yet I could see nothing out of the ordinary.

"I could have sworn I detected something on the aerials,

both high and low altitudes," I said out loud. "I'm sure I went in the right direction and the GPS just verified I'm the correct distance from camp."

I paused at that spot for five minutes or so trying to clear my head.

"Okay Eric, start thinking logically. Mark the spot you are at, then systematically grid out different areas from that point. Arbitrarily pick one hundred yards out. Use a compass heading and stick to it."

Pleased with my self imposed logic, I again spoke out loud to no one.

"It's nice when you can think things out."

Now I was thinking I must be really losing it. First I talk to myself, and now I'm even answering myself. Even that I guess is okay. It's when you talk to yourself and then ask what, I wasn't listening, Then you are really in trouble.

I gave myself a good chuckle.

I marked a point on the ground with a long stick in the dirt tying my white handkerchief on the top, then started my first leg, my eyes searching. Nothing, although I could have sworn I detected the faintest smell of fire smoke. "That's ridiculous, " I dismissed.

Arriving at one hundred yards distance I moved my position and started my return trip to my starting point. Again nothing. Thinking about my stereo viewing back at the map table I thought, *"Don't get discouraged Eric, your eyes have not deceived you yet. After all, it appeared to be only a small clearing in between the jungle canopy."*

Keeping my spirits up I began my third leg remembering in addition to view the jungle canopy for an opening. The jungle seemed unusually quiet and for some reason I got a funny sensation as if I was being watched. A similar feeling to when the jaguar was tracking me but not as ominous. I continued my trek and the same feeling stayed with me. *"That's odd,"* I thought, *"I don't often feel this uneasy."* I paused my steps momentarily listening. I heard and saw nothing. I laughed at myself thinking what can be more threatening then being stalked by a large jungle cat. *"Just my imagination,"* I mumbled to myself.

I resumed my walk another twenty or thirty yards and abruptly halted. My unexpected halt caught whatever was trailing me unawares. I definitely heard movement. My inner self said it wasn't an animal. Right away I thought of one of the guys was playing tricks with me. The sound was very close, too close. In fact, so close, I heard the steps behind me. I turned smiling hoping to catch one of my friends in the act. As I was in the process of turning I caught a glimpse of two human figures neither of which were my friends. Before I could react further I found myself surrounded by six, no seven men. Totally unrecognizable. By their dress I knew they were Mayan, but not like the Maya I was familiar with. Their style of dress was dated. It reminded me of the attire of the Mayans we found in the Turquoise mine. I was not knowledgeable enough to say what period, I just knew it was dated.

I froze, scanning with my eyes. Four of them had what appeared to be lances. With a more careful look they were old Spanish lance heads, still shinny and polished though it was obvious the shafts or poles were new with the lance heads lashed on with leather strapping. Before I could respond in any way all four threatening lances were pointed at me within inches. One of the seven, carrying no weapon cautiously approached me and with a swift hand movement stripped the GPS and compass from my hands. He uttered a low guttural sound and two others grabbed my arms pulling them together and lashed them with thin leather strips. I started to verbally protest but thought better of it, for now anyway. I was then pushed in a direction ninety degrees to my original walking trail. They were not too rough nor were they too gentle. Not many words were spoken, but it mattered not. I did not understand them.

We walked for what I guessed was a half mile on well delineated trails. Suddenly before me was what I must have seen on the aerials. A scattered grouping of buildings encircling two small flat topped pyramids. The jungle had been allowed to reclaim some of its own. It was obvious this was a lived in settlement, just not kept up as you would have expected. At least not what I would have expected for a Mayan settlement. All houses and buildings were accessible yet the jungle growth of underbrush and vines were allowed to blend. That must be the reason I had trouble seeing it on the photos.

I was roughly pushed forward to the larger of the two pyramids. By now there were at least three dozen people, both men and women gathering around me. From behind the larger pyramid came a striking figure. Tall, well muscled and draped with all sorts of fabric garments, even a scarf, if you will, of red feathers adorning neck and shoulders, matching a headdress of red feathers also. All bowed in his presence.

I was forcibly pushed to my knees before him. Words were exchanged between who, I assumed was the leader , and those who captured me. I understood nothing.   The head man than retreated behind the pyramid as I was taken to the other side of what was their open courtyard. I was tied rather tightly to a well worn stone post and left alone save for a few curiosity seekers who did not venture too close.

Once alone, my nerves settled a bit, and my heart rate slowed somewhat. I looked around and before me was a pyramid shaped platform about eight feet above ground level. I remembered seeing pictures of similar structures while doing research of the Maya way of life. Then it hit me, and hard. This was a raised sacrificial alter. On the flat top was a raised table large enough to hold a good sized man.

My heart started to beat a little faster again. Was this to be my fate ? Then something else caught my eye that, I must admit, frightened me even more. There were trailing blood stains from the platform, spilling down the steps to the level ground. They were dried but obviously recent. When I say recent, I don't mean within a few days but probably within months.

While my thoughts were preoccupied a lone man ascended the sacrificial alter to prepare for the time honored ceremony. He carried with him one of the Spanish Conquistador lance heads.

Now I was really panicking. My thoughts went right to Violet and how much I now knew I loved her.

Suddenly I realized I was left alone, which was comforting in a way. What do I do now? My mind was going a mile a minute with all kinds of thoughts but only confusing myself more.

"Are you alright Eric, I have a strong feeling of danger. Please tell me you are safe."

The sound of Violet's voice was suddenly uplifting, enough that I could think more clearly.

The king came to mind. If Violets thoughts took over my mind and filled me with wanting, this could or would be the key to my survival. I must contact the king. Fortunately it did not take long.

**"Your predicament frightens me Eric."**

"That's an understatement if I ever heard one," I thought.

"Can you help me ?" I pleaded. After a short pause he answered.

**"Use my name Eric and use the gift you have. It will bring the answers you seek."**

There he goes with the riddles again. Rather abruptly my head cleared and I knew what he meant. I now made up my mind to do two things. First and foremost I sent telepathic signals to my four Pals. I knew it was possible to cover great distances but whether or not my friends would be openly alert to such a message was questionable. I think and hope the king will be assisting along that line.

My second gamble was to send Dove of Spring a message that I was okay. Not exactly the truth but I was hoping to alleviate her fears. Next was a stretch but I figured I had nothing to lose, besides the king said to use his name. I was still alone so my thoughts were busy sending my SOS message. I concentrated like never before. Mario was the first to tune in. I explained briefly and gave directions. Diego also tuned to my outcry. These two, of course were the most familiar with the mental technique having been using it the longest. I repeated my dire situation over and over as if I was using a telegraph key.

I know I spent a lot of time in the thought process, exactly how long I couldn't say but I knew I was becoming fatigued.

I rested my mind a bit knowing help would be on the way. I just hoped it would be on time. In the meantime I again put to use the kings advice. One of my captors was approaching and when I thought he was within hearing range I looked straight at him and yelled "Atal".

He froze in his motion. In fact it almost made me laugh. It was like watching an old cartoon movie. He literally froze in position. He looked up, down and around, eyes in constant motion. When his head was turned away from me I yelled again, even louder. "ATAL"

Now there were others who were curious about the sound. Slowly they inched their way toward me. *"I hope I did the right thing."* came to mind or perhaps I would be meeting with an even earlier demise. I wish I knew more of the Mayan language or "Yucatecan" as Mario referred to it.

The king must have been reading my thoughts because his familiar echo entered my head.

"Eric, use my name again and follow with "K'awil" that should buy time. I am here my friend."

Without hesitation I voiced the words as instructed. I hoped I was pronouncing it correctly. I must have been close to right for everyone stopped their approach, frightened in place you might say. A few were conversing and pointing to the large pyramid where I first met who I assumed was the leader. Within seconds one man took off running to the pyramid.

It's funny when you think about it. Here I am, close to having my heart cut out on a sacrificial alter yet at the same time a sensation of excitement was flooding my body. *"Many people have often said I never was too right in the head."*

Not because of imminent death but being back in ancient history, living ancient history. Suddenly it became a surreal world.

This isolated group, most likely had never had contact with the outside world of today, or very little. I suddenly thought of them as being somewhat fortunate. They are living what my four friends and I are trying to study. How lucky can one man be.

"Get a hold of yourself again Eric, your thinking is turning weird once more."

A   large crowd following the head man was fast approaching.

"Why did I pick now to think about how hot it is in the sun. Usually I have some sort of shade to escape to. Come back to reality Eric," I scolded.

The grand robed man now stood before me, a curious

scowl on his face. I noticed he did not get too close. He spouted something incomprehensible as if asking a question. Calmly this time I repeated my two words. Shock and surprise showed on his face.

"Now what do I do ? Those are my only two words." I mumbled quietly to myself.

He remained silent, staring at me. At last he moved forward, the look on his face not as menacing. Lowering his voice a notch or two he repeated what he shouted earlier, at least it sounded the same. I looked at him shaking my head no. I repeated my two words followed with the shaking my head yes. I dared gazing directly into his questioning eyes watching them grow softer.

For whatever reason I felt the life threatening danger disappear. I felt I now had time. I just did not know how to use it to my advantage. We stood gaging each other neither one speaking. He mumbled something to one of his underlings who immediately turned and ran to the pyramid. I estimated six or seven minutes before his return. He was carrying a scepter, smaller than the kings yet recognizable. Magic sand was the first thing to enter my mind. I dismissed that idea almost instantly after seeing the way it was being handled.

The chief, or whatever he was called now held the scepter, I was assuming it was a sign of rank. With another step closer he said my two words back to me. He then smiled somewhat and nodded his head yes. I followed suit with a head nod and returned the smile.

Satisfied with himself he turned to his followers saying Atal and at the same time pointing to me.

Now I was worried once more. I had no way of telling them I was not Atal. On word from their leader a few came forward and untied me, bowing and uttering words I have never heard.

I rubbed my arms and wrists to get the blood circulating once more. I was escorted with respect to the leader who immediately bowed before me. He stayed in that position till I realized it was up to me to indicate for him to stand upright again. He did so with a welcoming smile. He repeated my two words again smiling and pointing to me and looking at the rather large gathering.

I was racking my brains for ways to convince him I was not Atal. I called for the kings help. I did get an answer just not what I expected.

"You need not my help Eric. Others are here."

I searched around seeing nothing encouraging. About to call on the king again a familiar voice rang out, not in English but I knew the voice well.

Mario continued speaking as he drew closer. The crowd of ancient people slowly separated allowing Mario and my three other friends through to me. Now all four were talking to individuals. Mario was now with the leader and speaking somewhat forcibly with a deep and strong voice. The leader reacted as if he were being chastised. He bowed to Mario and slowly backed away a few feet.

Mario , holding himself erect looked over the gathered crowd. He turned a full three hundred and sixty degrees all the time keeping a serious face.

Approaching me slowly he bowed, whispering "Just follow my lead." Still bowing I heard him murmur "Okay, you can let me up now."

Smiling at and almost wanting to laugh, I used my right arm to indicate he should rise. I noticed my other friends remained at the outer fringe of the settlement. They were also being viewed suspiciously as if they also were sacred Gods.

Mario, still whispering, instructed me to walk to Carlos and the others.

"Try to do it in a stately manner. I will follow shortly. Continue with them into the jungle. Don't worry I will catch up eventually."

I did as Mario suggested, trying to remember the demeanor of the king when he walked with us. Apparently I was doing okay, the gathering parted allowing me to pass. Most even bowed avoiding my eyes.

I reached my three companions who bowed there heads slightly and the four of us disappeared into the green curtain of trees.

It was not until we were safely out of sight that we stopped to the smiling faces of my comrades.

"That was a close one." stated Diego. "Now we're glad

you have such great contacts with the king. It would not have been a good thing to see you sacrificed, especially when there is still so much more you have to discover for us."

Even I laughed along on that.

"Never mind future discoveries. Look what you have just found," Carlos said excitedly, which was not his normal behavior. "Here we all are trying to dig up old history the hard way and you find Ancient history as living history. From what I have just observed I would venture a guess as late post classic peoples. This is going to be one hell of a story if we play everything just right. But that, right now is secondary. The prime concern right now is your safety and welfare. Are you alright ?"

Smiling and happy that I still could, I answered affirmatively.

I slowly related my whole mornings activity.

"How did you get released ?" Mateo asked hurriedly.

"Atal told me to use his name and then follow it with "K'awil"."

This strange word stopped the three Mayans for a moment. They looked at me, questions filled their eyes

"The best I could make of it was they thought I was Atal. I believe that was the only reason they freed me from my bonds."

"At least that proves they know about the king," Diego threw out.

"Now I'm the curious one," I remarked. "Why are you bowing to me, besides the fact that I deserve it." I smiled as I got hit by all three. "Seriously though, why the bowing ?"

Carlos answered for the group. "That was the kings idea. Apparently he felt more comfortable talking to Mario in your absence, therefore he made that suggestion. I think he knew they would react to his name and the word that followed."

"That word that I followed with, what was it or what does it mean ?"

"I'll let Mario explain the details of it, but it has reference to the Gods and even could reference a scepter. It depends on how it is combined with other words."

I smiled and answered, "Thanks, that makes it as clear as mud to me."

Carlos admitted he was not far behind in that thinking.

It was another twenty minutes before Mario rejoined us. In the meantime I was asked all sorts of questions regarding my physical well being. They were truly concerned for my welfare. Once my physical integrity was established I again became the brunt of their jokes .

Mario finally joined the discussion in an extremely excited manner,

"I can't believe what we just witnessed today. Actual living history," he voiced animatedly. "This group of people are continuing life of at least eight hundred to a thousand years ago. They have been living in isolation like that by choice. They are remembering the old days, before the Spanish. They have agreed to talk further as long as Atal or his emissary is present."

He said this looking directly at me.

"Why are you looking at me ?" I asked in a guilty fashion.

He answered with the obvious.

"They already think you are Atal, because you told them that."

"I didn't say anything of the kind. All I did was say the words that Atal gave me, his name and one other word."

"As I said." smiled Mario. "You told them that you were Atal. That other word by the way, is used in conjunction with certain names indicating rank, title Sovereignty, etc. So you are Atal or his emissary. Remember when the leader repeated your words and shook his head yes, well you followed suit admitting you were that designated person. So to keep the charade up we bowed to you."

"It is what it is Eric" interrupted Carlos. "As much as I do not like deceiving others I suggest we use this situation to our advantage. When else are we going to get a chance to actually live history of a thousand years ago. I'm not suggesting we live with them but we should visit frequently."

Mario joined the conversation again.

"I can converse with them but it is rather difficult. Some

of their words are a mix of old and older language stems. Some of which I have very little familiarity with, yet I think we will be able to manage, especially with the "Chosen One" at our side."

With that all four pair of eyes were on me.

"Ahh, come on guys, I was just trying to save my hide. I only said what the king told me to say."

Mario suggested the Chosen One should return to camp for a good rest and some food. He would return to the settlement, along with Diego. He would not take long and would follow us to camp shortly.

I was feeling physically okay while my thoughts were all over the place, yet I was looking forward to the comfort of our camp. There is no place like home as the saying goes.

During the quiet walk back to base the king paid another visit,

"I am pleased to see you are well Eric. My people meant you no real harm. They were just shocked by your intrusion into their peaceful universe. Their memories and legends only tell of evil times brought by strangers from across the sea. Hardships of slaughter and mistrust have never been forgotten. They are as children who have yet to learn compared to you. As you are a child compared to my knowledge. Accept their mistrust for what it is and be patient. Teach them what you can but do not force the knowledge. They will turn you away as you turned me away. Remember, let patience be your guide and let them exist in harmony with nature and the way of the universe."

As his voice trailed off I realized we were back at camp, though the wisdom of his words still echoed in my being. When we five are together tonight I will relay the kings words as I understood them. I was now truly feeling comfortable with myself.

Violet will be my first priority once settled for the evenings serenade.

It was almost two and a half hours and approaching darkness when our two comrades returned. They were both smiling and appeared highly inspired. The three of us welcomed them and waited open mouthed for their good news. We were ignored when Mario, straight faced, asked,

"What! Supper's not ready yet ?"

"What have you guys been doing all day ?" Diego threw in as he helped himself to water.

Carlos mumbled,

"It's a wonder we ever get anything done. We never talk to each other."

He said this trying to hide his grin, unsuccessfully.

Mario plopped himself down at the table all smiles.

"Okay, I'm ready to talk, but I am really hungry. Remember the "Chosen One" here deprived us of lunch just to save his sorry butt. By the way oh careless one, I found these in the jungle on the way back here. You should be more careful with your toys."

Mario handed Eric his GPS and compass.

"And here's your handkerchief you left flying on a pole in the jungle. You know there are littering laws here also." added Diego.

Their comments set the mood for a great evening. We let Mario and Diego rest as we prepared a quick dinner. I was sorry I did not have any Cognac left. I believe we all deserved a reward.

Dinner was quick and easy while no one seemed to notice or care. We were too involved in the happenings of the day.

Mario reported that it was a definite conclusion that the people of the settlement believed I was the "Chosen One". Not necessarily Atl but one of high ranking. Enough that they would most likely adhere to whatever I said.

Suddenly I felt a heavy burden on my shoulders. I was not their leader nor did I have any desire to be so. My mood change must have shown on my facial expression and was noticed by my companions.

Carlos, taking his usual serious lead was the first to speak,

"Try not to take this so seriously Eric. We are in this together and we will work this out. We know how you feel about the

"Chosen One" charade, but we will all do this as one."

The others chimed in, one by one reaffirming Carlos's statement.

"To us of course we know you are that special one but we won't let on to the settlement residents," commented Mario with a smile of course.

I must admit Carlos's words did help settle me somewhat.

Mario asserted himself again.

"Let me finish my tale of our visit before we go any further, please." he commented

We agreed that was the right thing and settled back to listen. Mario then outlined their short visit with interjections from Diego with much enthusiasm. They were shown a few dwellings and the inside of the larger pyramid which was sacred to them. Because of their studies both Mario and Diego knew how to react and handle their visit as if they were part of this isolated group. Mario did say the "Chosen One" would visit again if only to encourage their continuance in their way of life. All five of us would visit from time to time until our mission called us elsewhere. Diego then added that they welcomed this whole heartedly and looked forward to visits from the "Chosen One".

The table was silent now all waiting for Eric's input.

Knowing all eyes were on him and the team patiently waiting, Eric sipped his coffee and slowly sat back.

"Okay guys, I am really pleased with what has taken place so far. Let me give you my input then you decide what you have to do. We are all here for the same thing, to further our understanding of the past. This, of course, is a unexpected gift to study the living past. But I caution us to do so without disturbing their way of living. We should not force our world or ways on them. Nor do I feel we should deceive them in any way, you know by promising them false hope. If you think we can achieve these goals while learning what we can with the least disturbance, then I say let's try. But again I caution, if you think this cannot be achieved without a change in their lives then I for one say let them be."

A hush fell over the table once again. Slowly, one by one the four Mayan friends broke into smiles.

"**P**erhaps you are a "Chosen One" stated Carlos softly with a true smile.

"**Y**ou are definitely a Mayan," voiced Mateo.

Eric could feel himself blushing which he tried to hide by sipping at his coffee mug.

The chatter became active once more with all agreeing with Eric's thoughts. The subject now being how to act and dress when visiting their new found settlement. They all spoke of discouraging any visits by the people to their encampment here.

Their plan being basically laid out the discussion turned to a more detailed day by day routine, keeping visits to only a few a week. It was also agreed no pictures would be taken. As disappointed as Eric was he agreed that it was the right decision.

Minor suggestions were then talked over till all agreed bedtime would be the next best thing for the day.

Eric could not wait to contact Dove of Spring, which he did quite easily much to his surprise.

"I feel you are safe now my love but I must admit I had my doubts earlier. I know you have desires to fulfill, and I agreed to let you go, but please Darling hurry back to me. I have a strong need for you and I to be us again. Sweet dreams."

With that Violet was gone leaving Eric with a few tears and an empty feeling. Empty on one hand yet fulfilling on the other.

His serenade of the night took him away to a peaceful sleep.

Chapter 16

Along with the screaming monkeys came a friendly voice.

"You have done well, my young friend. Your meeting with my ancient children went well. You will learn much. I am aware of your wise council to your friends and I am pleased. I myself will add to your words later when you partake of your morning repast. You may alert your friends."

The usual hollow fading took place. Eric lay there in h_s hammock a smile on his face. He whispered a quick good morning to Violet remembering her words of last night and smiled as he went about his morning routine rather cheerfully.

It was now going on eight o'clock and all were gathered at the breakfast table, the usual chatter between laughs. Once settled with a pause in conversation Eric announced the kings message.

There was a sudden silence.

Carlos spoke quietly.

"This must really be important to speak to all of us at once. Did he say when ?"

"No' I answered. "Just that he said when we were all gathered at breakfast."

No sooner when Eric ended his sentence when the king

tuned into all five.

"My friends, I am honored to be in your presence once again. You have my trust and admiration."

An unknown quiet overcame the jungle. Even the monkeys went silent. Another few moments of stillness reigned. Finally the king resumed his promised message.

This settlement and other small groups managed to avoid the Spanish and English terror campaigns. They hid their treasured possessions, as you are finding now. Their treasures, as you are well aware now, were not for wealth, but for beauty and tribute to the Gods. Their religion was all but destroyed. These small bands of survivors chose isolation which is why they still appear somewhat backwards to you. They are anything but. They still have their writing, their art, their knowledge of the stars, and medicine. I could go on for hours as you well know. Your technological advancements are not necessarily correct for all peoples. Compare yourselves with them. I do not mean just you five. I mean your total society. Do you live in peaceful co-existence with one another ? Are you preserving the environment ? Are you sharing your environment with all ? Are you safeguarding the animals for future survival ? Is your success shared with those less fortunate ? Your thinking and that of your companions is following a correct path to success for all. That, as you have already learned, puts you in a very small minority in this world of today. These few groups may not have the success of wealth as you know it but they already possess the very things you aspire to but slowly discard as your technology advanced.

You alone Eric, enjoy the symphonic music of the jungle, as you call it. It leaves you with total peace and happiness. You missed it when you left these environs. That same stressless environment is the always world of these people. The land feeds them, clothes them and provides all that is necessary for life, their life, their happy life. Why then is it always necessary for the outsiders, who consider themselves advanced, to force their ways on people who already have the ways for peace and harmony. Technological advances do not necessarily mean happiness or advancement. I'm talking of true happiness. The kind that fills the very core of your being. Do your machines and computers make the sunset more beautiful ? Do they enhance the whisper of the breeze in the treetops? Do they make the babbling brook any more inviting ? Can they make you love one another more ? Do they put a stop to destructive wars or start them ? Do they do away with greed and the need for power or do they enhance the desire for such things.

The study of ancient peoples, such as these that you have come upon, has not taught man of today anything. The lessons of life are before you but you do not see. Think about your studies and learn from them. Seek your own method of happiness and then teach others.

I am pleased and honored by your decision of yesterday not to interfere with these people. Learn from them what you need but do not deceive. I will always be here to help when needed. Remember, your future is really from your past"

That sound of hollow emptiness took over all five minds,

The king was no longer there.

As if by some sort of silent signal the familiar sounds of the jungle returned to normal.

~ ~ ~ ~ ~ ~

Eric and his four Mayan friends remained silent, each digesting the kings words. The only disturbance of the area was the quiet noise of the jungle. That silence reigned for more than five minutes.

"Who can argue with those words," Mateo uttered quietly to no one in particular.

Carlos followed with,

"No wonder Eric gets along with the king so well."

The ice of quietude now being broken the five comrades were again wearing smiles.

"I don't know about you guys but I'm going back to my exciting documentation paper work today. Yesterday was much too boring a day," offered Diego subtly as he poured a second cup of coffee.

Of course there were laughs all around but the consensus was the same. By previous agreement there would not be too many visits to the settlement.

"We all have our chosen work. What about you Eric ? Have you made any plans for the day ?"

"Not really, but I was considering going back to the Golden Lady's tomb tomorrow to investigate the other three sides for anything that we may have missed."

Suddenly they were all in accordance with his thinking.

"What a great idea. That will give us a break from the doldrums of paperwork," volunteered Mario.

"Not only that, but it will give us a chance to keep an eye on Eric and keep him out of trouble, " jested Mateo.

"That settles it then." threw in Diego. "I will stay in camp and fix dinner. I want to catch up on some sketching anyway."

"So much for being alone, " smiled Eric.

Chapter   17

    Diego was up before the sun and had scratched up breakfast to every ones satisfaction. He was already on his way to the kings tomb, sketch pad and all, as the others were just stirring. Breakfast was quick with the usual joviality, then the four of us set to work gathering what we thought would be the necessities for the days search. Each checked the others gatherings and agreed all was in readiness.

    The walk to the trapezoidal tomb was fast paced and silent. Each man lost in their own thoughts.

    "I admire your attention to the continued search Eric."

    The kings voice startled Eric who was deeply involved in memories of Dove of Spring. He quickly looked to the others.

    Anticipating this the king remarked.

    "Do not worry my friend. My words are for you alone. Just remember, the success of the search is best if continued in a straight line."

    The normal hollow echo followed the last word. Eric just smiled to himself thinking that the riddles will probably never stop.

    As they approached the flat topped pyramid Eric let the others go ahead while he again studied the outer wall. He was still fascinated by the faux trees intertwined with the live ones. "And we call ourselves advanced." he thought. He never ceased to be amazed by the resourcefulness of the ancients.

He caught up to his friends as they were discussing the digging process and where to start. It then dawned on Eric the meaning of the kings riddle. He explained the kings remarks and strongly suggested they start on the opposite side of the structure from that of the Golden Lady's tomb. They all agreed, with Carlos giving an extra broad smile.

"**D**on't ever get the king angry, " he commented. "We'll never find another thing."

Settled on their chosen side they located the same rectangular platform as the entrance to the other side. All four pitched in and soon had exposed a similar descending staircase. Not as well designed but adequate for their purpose.

Carlos looked to Eric as if asking permission which was quickly answered with an affirmative head nod. Carlos then took the first step down as Mario and Mateo smiled to each other.

"**T**oo bad the whole world doesn't get along this way, " softly said Mateo.

The three followed Carlos carefully watching the steps on the unknown stairway. Carlos had stopped at a roughly constructed door of an unknown heavy hardwood. It took longer than usual to find the hidden trigger when the click was finally heard. It sounded more like a loud thunk. The heavy roar of the door movement caught everyone's attention which only heightened the anticipation. Their lanterns revealed a totally different interior passageway. Smooth walls covered with a soft brownish yellow pigment. Not really identifiable as paint or ornamental coating.

"**L**et's leave that for later study," Carlos remarked. "That would be more up Diego's ally anyway.

The group slowly moved forward taking note of a slight angular turn to the right which showed an even longer hallway. Torches were located about every twenty feet along the wall. They were small but apparently provided enough light for the user. We chose not to use them, this trip anyway.

As expected another door showed itself. Carlos froze before it, staring unbelieving. All lanterns were now highlighting the door and symbol unreadable to any of us was this Chinese like character. More than Chinese like, it was a Chinese character. I had seen the same symbol on the trade contracts in the desert.

Carlos quietly asked, "Can you read it?"

"No." I answered in the same low voice. "But it was a common marking on all the trading contracts that dealt with the Oriental."

You could tell the excitement was building in each of us yet no one moved towards the door/

"This is crazy, almost unreal. Here we are looking for our ancestors history but who expected the Chinese," Carlos commented.

"Or the Egyptians," added Mateo.

I quietly smiled to myself. After the last three years of what I have been exposed to, nothing really surprised me anymore. I think I would accept what ever turned up, no matter what part of the world it came from. It sort of proves what little we really know of our worlds history.

Mario's patience finally ran out.

"Okay, why are we just standing here. We came here for a reason. So let's just do it. Can you open the door Carlos ?"

"I'll try." he replied in an almost annoyed voice.

He turned back to the large stone before him and put his fingers to work. He scratched quietly for close to five minutes with no luck. You could tell he was frustrated. He tried again with the same " no go" results.

"Typical of the Chinese, they have to make everything into a puzzle."

As he said this he kicked at the bottom of the stone door. Mario was about to offer some calming words when sounds of stone grinding on stone struck our ears as we watched the door pivot open.

"Well, that's a new one on me." imparted Carlos with an embarrassed smile.

We all pretended not to notice his embarrassment with our eyes fixed on the opening. The door opened outward and to our left revealing nothing more than a space we would call a large closet. We stood there with our mouths open in disbelief. I guess we were expecting too much after our Golden Lady's throne room.

We slowly moved into the closet space with barely enough

room for the four of us. Once properly illuminated what we saw were familiar stacks of shelves holding small scrolls. It was almost a duplicate of the library room, as we called it, in the kings tomb. We were really stymied now. Mario was the first to reach for one of the scrolls. Unrolled it was only about fifteen or sixteen inches long.

"This looks like one of your contracts Eric."

I looked over his shoulder and confirmed his assumption. Each of us then grabbed a few scrolls. They were all contracts. The only difference this time was that Mario and Mateo both said they could read parts of them.

It was decided that we remove a few to take back with us to camp for closer inspection and decipherment. I again confirmed that they were the same as those we discovered in the desert.

I was a bit puzzled by this discovery, expecting more. I backed away from the others hoping to contact the king. As usual he was one step ahead of me.

Comfortably away from the others, the king anticipating my questions, went into his riddle mode.

"Disappointed you should not be. Remember other places. Seek and you shall find."

Of course there was the trailing voice and I knew he was gone.

Trying not to act too obvious I inched my way back into the stone closet.

"Hey guys," I spoke quietly. "Did you notice anything funny about this room ?"

In return I received inquiry stares.

"I'm talking about the short distance from the entrance to where we are. We are no where near the center of this mysterious structure. Do you think, perhaps, there is still other rooms ?"

Instantly accepting my suggestion Mateo and Mario exited the closet and were checking the outer walls on either side of the door.

"The king still playing games again ?" asked Carlos with a smile.

I did not answer but just returned his smile.

The pair of us turned to the shelves and started checking the back wall.

It wasn't long when Carlos softly muttered,

"Well looky here."

With that I could hear sliding stone once more. It was becoming a familiar sound to all of us. We could see a wide entranceway behind the shelves. Both thinking the same thing we reached for the shelving, which quite easily parted like doors leaving a more than adequate passage. By now the other two had rejoined us.

"Okay Mateo," I said with a grin. "Your turn to make a discovery."

His broad smile betrayed his pleasure and without hesitation he stepped forward and through the portal his lantern raised. We all waited to give him some time before we followed.

"It turns sharply to the right." Was Mateo's echoing comment.

A few minutes of silence before he spoke again.

"Time for Carlos to do his thing."

He obviously came to a wall or blocked doorway. We caught up with him and he was still smiling at being the first.

We faced an apparent doorway or so it appeared. Wearing a joking grin Carlos kicked the wall first then stood back.

"Nothing. Okay now I'll look." he said yet smiling.

It did not take long before the opening appeared. Again we all stepped back to allow Mateo first glance. We were looking at a room about twenty feet square with a sort of domed ceiling that had to be at least fifteen feet high. We lit the provided torches on the wall. Once properly illuminated our eyes feasted on stacks and stacks of neatly folded silks, all colors and designs. These piles lined the whole inner wall to a height of maybe ten feet. The middle of the room displayed a table holding all sorts of curios. The first thing our eyes settled on was a ship. An ancient Chinese ship. Most likely a to scale model as was the Egyptian ship. To scale or not to scale it was an impressive model. I had to laugh to myself at the mouth open expressions of my three companions. As trained as they were there was still a bit of a shock witnessing Far East contact.

Mario took some Polaroid pictures for Diego's benefit. This would really drive him nuts.

"I had no idea, "uttered Mateo. "But how did they get so far inland ?"

"With the help of your ancestors," replied Carlos.

Mario next posed, "I can understand sailing to the west coast but to get here on the east would be a challenge."

"You must remember, the Chinese navy was the most impressive of its time. One of their Admirals, I think Zeng Hi was his name, was even reported to have sailed to Europe and did some trade exchanges with Italy."

"How do you know all this ?" asked Mateo.

"I just read a lot" was my simple answer.

"If you read that much, how do you find time to do anything else ?" He queried in return.

"Just lucky I guess," I shot back with a smile.

We all went about the business of looking, feeling, admiring the stacks before our eyes. In today's market these silks would command a small fortune but that was not our quest or desire. Their historical value meant more to us. These were obviously trade goods. But trade for what ? Jade possibly. But the Chinese had there own jade. Or was the Yucatan jade more unique. Something we will probably never know. At least not in our lifetime.

The Chinese were also advanced in astronomy. Was this part of the trade visit ? Were these two very different cultures exchanging ideas ?   I think all of us were examining this question in our own minds. Would the answer ever show itself ? That we would most likely never know.

We continued with our fascination with the Chinese silks.

"This sure puts a definite detour in the silk road of history," I thought to myself. There wasn't much more of interest in this silk hideaway. We had seen it all, twice over, which still left many questions. It turned out apparently to just be a storeroom. I think I was the first one to quit actually looking.

I decided to remind the others that there was still two more sides to this structure to investigate but based on the words of the king earlier I doubt we would find anything.

"Just remember, the success of the search is best if continued in a straight line."

At least that was my interpretation of the kings riddle speak. Perhaps I am getting used to his riddles, heaven forbid.

Verbally I spoke my mind, " Okay guys we still have two other sides to look into, I really don't think there is much else to find here. What say we at least look at one more before it gets dark." All were in agreement.

"What he really wants is for us to do the digging for him," said a smiling Mateo.

"I didn't think you would figure that out," I answered. "Okay, just for that I and I alone will do the digging and you three can watch and see how a professional does it."

We closed up the silk closet and slowly proceeded to the ninety degree side to the left of the structure. I started to clear some dirt away to expose the platform door. As I did this the other three made themselves comfortable sitting or half lying on the ground putting themselves in a perfect position to watch me. There was no attempt or even a suggestion of helping me. I decided to see how far this joke would play out so I made no attempt to appear disturbed or act with hurt feelings. It proves that they also were playing the same game.

"Oh well," I thought. *"I guess that's what real friends do."*

I ignored them and seriously concentrated on my digging. I actually felt good doing it. After another five minutes or so Carlos spoke out.

"I just remembered guys. Eric is supposed to fix dinner tonight. At this rate he won't be able to. As much as we don't want to, we better pitch in with this hole in the ground."

Within seconds my three friends were digging away.

As expected, after about a two foot depth there was

nothing but rocks and jungle rubble. It was agree that further effort would result in nil.

This still allowed us a short time to try the last side. Carlos and I moved there to dig while Mario and Mateo filled in and covered our previous digging efforts.

By the time they rejoined us we were already under way refilling our meager dis-rupture of this fourth side. They aided in making our trenching of the earth disappear.

We began our homeward trek looking forward to dinner. We still chatted about our silk discovery but it lacked the drive and exciting drama of the revelation of the Golden Lady. It was a discovery that was almost anticlimactic. As important as this find was, connecting the Chinese to the Maya, it was disappointing and I think we all felt this. We were spoiled by past revelations and expected each new one to out do the others. But let's face it, that was not reality.

We arrived back at home base just in time for the orchestral change. My night time symphony was just beginning. Tonight it would just have to wait.

Diego had dinner waiting as we all expected. Of course he had to include his usual dramatic wit.

"I was just about to call the local sherif to report you missing. I already started working on a schedule on how I could finish this research by myself."

Of course he said this with his ever present smile and laughing eyes.

Carlos, on one of his rare non-serious moments answered immediately,

"Good, show me the schedule, I'll help you work on it then we four can leave and go home where there aren't any screeching monkeys."

This caught all of us by surprise, particularly Diego, who was not expecting a serious answer. It took a few seconds but he finally caught on that Carlos was just playing his same game.

We put away our equipment and rejoined at the table for chow. Diego out did himself again. He had gone fishing and was quite lucky with his catch. We all proceeded to stuff ourselves without talking, listening only to the jungle sounds.

Finally, after finishing what Diego had prepared, we sat back, still tired but with totally sated appetites. Diego still in his comic mode, spoke sadly,

"Thanks guys. After struggling all day to get a good dinner, you could have at least allowed me to have some."

Carlos, yet in a humorous bent answered,

"You don't have time for meals. Remember you now have to do the work of five. We are going to start packing now."

Diego all smiles now unwrapped another two fish.

"Just in case some one wanted a third helping."

He laughed as he fed himself.

Mario was the first to break down.

"We have a present for you Pal." he said as he reached for his pack. He pulled out the Polaroid picture of the Chinese ship model to the delight of Diego. He was even too excited to speak.

"How- - - Where - - - When- - - can I see it ?"

He seemed to say all at once. We at last settled down and related the whole days story. He was even more excited by the Chinese silks and the China connection.

Chapter 18

The wonder of when all this took place was on everybody's mind.

"I just don't understand how we never came across these connections before," Mario quizzed.

"The treasure room" I blurted out.

The other four looked at me as if I lost my marbles. I smiled and continued in a more normal voice.

"I just remembered the treasure room in the kings tomb."

Stares that still showed skepticism led me to further explain.

"When we were all taking a mental, inventory after it was found I came across a large gold "ANK", definitely Egyptian, as were a few other objects. We sort of dismissed them at the time. I think because of being distracted by the immensity of the whole room."

Questioning eyes still gazed at Eric.

Half smiling he further explained.

"We never really identified any objects from China but that doesn't mean there weren't any. That treasure trove is so immense we truly don't know what is there or from where."

Nods of understanding spread onto the others.

"Eric's right, we never did complete an inventory, what with Frank's incident and the season coming to an end." Mario offered.

He was about to continue when Diego innocently interrupted,

"Why not ask those who may still remember ?"

Now it was my turn to join the others in not understanding what he meant. Diego still had his eyes buried in the picture of the Chinese sailing ship. He looked up because of the sudden silence.

"Oh," he said almost laughing. "The village not far from here. You know, the ones who wanted to sacrifice Eric." He laughed softly. "Since they have not been tainted by modern times, they may still remember some of the old tales, you know our oral history."

As he finished speaking he went right back to the he held.

We all sat there a bit chagrined. Diego had come up with the perfect and most logical answer. The keeping of oral history and passing down the tales had always been a major part of Maya culture. The possibility of that age old connection to outsiders may still exist with the untouched group.

Mario was the first to caution us.

"We are still strangers to these people. I for one would not want to destroy their world as it exists today. If we all agree to pursue this quest we must plan it carefully so as not to change their life style."

We all instantly agreed with Mario. We must handle this with total respect for their present culture and innocence.

Our group remained silent for a time each thinking of a possible approach. Carlos, again in his logical air broke the group trance,

"What we are considering is a major undertaking. Perhaps not for us but for these ancestral peoples. We should not do this with haste. Results along those lines could be devastating to their innocence. The hour is late and we need our rest. Tomorrow we will have clearer heads. Let us all reflect on this idea for a time before we jump to a conclusion that could be detrimental to both groups; us and them."

His wisdom was readily accepted with smiles of acknowledgment.

I for one was extremely happy with our mutual decision. I was anxious to get to my hammock and tell Violet of our discovery.

All pitched in on cleanup and each parted for their own sleeping area.

~ ~ ~ ~ ~

My nighttime symphony was well under way by the time I closed the mosquito netting. My thoughts directly focused on Dove of Spring with a strong desire to make a successful connection. I reviewed our days adventure and received an immediate response. I was so happy I almost spoke out loud. Our connection was short lived yet I was pleased with what we did have. Our love for each other was exchanged before our mental telephone was disrupted. I drifted off to a pleasant sleep almost counting the days for my return to her Navajo world.

~ ~ ~ ~ ~

We were all up at the same time thanks to our screeching monkey friends though we took it in stride knowing we were the intruders. I made the coffee while Carlos and Mateo managed a nice variety of fruit for our morning repast.

Conversation at breakfast was light and plans for a thorough work day were made. No mention was made about a visit to the ancients. We were all still working things out individually to contribute collectively to a successful plan.

I was to go with Diego back to the silk find. He, like a child, could not wait to see the model Chinese ship. We were also going to analyze the coloring of the passageway wall to the silk room. As Carlos said, that was more his expertise. The other three would continue with mapping, sketching and recording of all the finds to date. A detailed and well rounded presentation of the city was definitely needed if others were to follow in the future. My mapping and discovery of the underground tunnel was also going to be included in the overall presentation. We agreed our final report would read more like a book than a scientific presentation knowing we would be facing a lot of doubting minds once we released our findings. My friends were also counting on my photographic analyses to help win over the doubting Thomases. We also were counting on my Navajo friends research and findings to coincide with our final presentation, but those things were still far off.

It turned out to be a very productive day for us all with no new challenges. Just good old hard work. Actually it was very rewarding.

Diego was able to analyze the pigment on the wall of the silk room passageway and determined it was from local trees. Sort of a

stucco made from the sap and bark. His journal report on this kept him busy
up till bedtime. He even worked on it through dinner. It was a big journal
night for all but not a burdensome task.

Chapter 19

We chose to work through a few more days of just plain recording work. We even surprised ourselves with how much we actually accomplished. I myself helped them as much as possible and only spent a few scattered hours with the air photos. I did not find any new obvious anomalies but then again I wasn't looking very hard.

For whatever reason I returned to camp mid-afternoon one day only to find the others had done the same. I guess it was mutual intuition.

Carlos was the first one back and appeared happy to see us all early. We gathered around the coffee pot as was our habit when he asked us to join him at the table. Once seated he addressed us in a serious tone,

"I think it's time now to make our plans to visit the ancient village. That is if we still want to pursue this. I'm sure you all have some thoughts on this so let's put everything on the table."

I volunteered to go first with the obvious.

"I don't think all five of us should go together. That could cause some suspicions."

We all nodded in agreement to that.

"The most obvious choice, in my opinion, would be Mario, since he is the best of you in the use of their language."

No one disagreed with this, not even Mario. Carlos asserted himself once more.

"And of course you must go."

I started to object when Carlos raised his hand to stop me.

Quietly speaking he provided his reason.

"You know this is true. After all you represent the "ATL", or at least they think you do."

"That makes sense Eric, and you know it," interjected Mateo.

Smiling, but not wanting to, I had to agree. He was right of course. That's what kept me from the sacrificial alter. I quietly sat back. They all were smiling at me now.

Carlos continued "Mateo, I think you should also go. Your knowledge of the Glyph's may come in handy. Diego and I will stay in the jungle nearby in case of trouble."

Carlos saying the word trouble startled me some what though the others appeared not to be disturbed at all. We sat quietly for a few moments till Diego animatedly spoke up,

"Of course you can't wear the clothes you are presently wearing. We got away with it once but I doubt we can a second time."

I don't know what the others were thinking but I felt Diego was right on with that statement. Before I could find my voice Carlos confirmed Diego's thoughts.

"I was just going to get to that very thing," he said. "We must get you three dressed accordingly. It won't be too difficult for Mario and Mateo because they are Maya, but our newly adopted son from up north should be made up a little better."

All eyes were now on me.

"Thanks guys, I feel like I'm in the hot box now."

They all laughed with me.

"Okay", I said jokingly. "I'll change my clothes, I'll even take a bath in the river if you want, but what do I wear ?"

"If I remember correctly, " joined Mateo, "The king had some additional robes in the room off the main part of the tomb. You were both about the same size."

"Great!" added Carlos. "That should do just fine."

"What about the scepter ?" asked Mario. "That should really add to the believability factor."

I thought about this for a while and felt I should put out my feelings.

"I don't know about you gentlemen, but I feel a little twinge of guilt doing this dress up thing. Isn't this being a little deceitful. Weren't they deceived enough by the Spaniards of long ago."

I guess I hit a sore spot with my friends. They all took on extremely serious faces. I'm guessing they had not considered that point. I knew their intentions were honorable and they were just trying to gather historical knowledge yet I was uncomfortable to try and pass myself off as their king of ages past.

"Sorry guys I'm not trying to put a damper on things but I am feeling a little guilt at this deception thing."

Carlos, as usual, jumped right in.

"You are absolutely correct my friend. Forgive me for being so insensitive to our brethren of old. We should have known better."

The other three seconded Carlos's words. My mind was operating at sonic speed while they were agreeing with me. When it became quiet again I looked at them and smiled,

"However, I may have a compromise solution."

Smiles, though guarded, returned to their faces. I paused , just teasing them.

"Well !" they all shouted in unison.

"Sorry guys, I just couldn't resist."

"Don't worry, we'll get you back." laughed Mario.

"My suggestion is that I will try and contact the king and get his thoughts on our plan which I'm sure he knows already."

"Try to do that as soon as possible," mentioned Carlos; "So we can plan our moves accordingly."

That went without saying as far as I was concerned. I just hoped the king would be cooperative.

A positive air took hold of our group and all was well again. We looked froward to the king's council.

Chapter 20

Eric separated himself from the others by returning to his hammock. He definitely wanted to contact Violet also. But first things first he thought as he lay back and made himself comfortable. He dared not close his eyes for fear of drifting off to sleep. The sleep thought barely finished when he heard the familiar voice of the king.

"I am pleased with your concern for the ancient ones Eric. I must say though, I am not surprised. You continue your behavior as a Chosen One."

"There he goes again." I thought to myself.

"Please do not berate me my fiend. I am only stating the obvious. There will come a time when you will accept your destiny. I will say no more at this time."

Eric knew by the voice tone that the topic was now closed. After a silent pause by both men the king spoke again as if the other subject had never occurred.

"Your consideration is well founded. As advanced as these people are in some things, they are babes by comparison to the thinking of your time period. Treat them as

such but without belittling them. They are more than your equals."

"My main concern, as you well know I'm sure, is not wanting to deceive them in any way. To me that does not bode well for our professional research."

"Again, Eric, you show your caring my friend, and that pleases me."

"My question then Atl, is shall we continue with our proposed plan or can your guidance show us a better way. We are only looking for historical tie ins, we mean not to change their life style."

"I have listened to your colleagues plans and can find no harm being put forth. You and your friends are working from your hearts. No purer science can be achieved than that. Dressing in more traditional apparel will be a productive thing. The proposal of the scepter is, by all means, an excellent one. I do not find deceit in its use. Your intentions are pure. It, as we both know, no longer has any power, but its symbolic status should be most helpful. Do not abuse that status, as I know you will not.

You, representing the king, do not have to say much. Allow Mario to do the conversing. I would also suggest Diego escort you rather than Mateo. True, Mateo has the Glyph knowledge but Diego's winning smile and manner will go a long way with these people. No disfavor towards Mateo is meant by this.

Have Mario also teach you a few key words that will then allow him to be the official spokesperson. Play your part with total humility. Instruct the others in the same mood. You will find the results much to your liking and

I was just about to thank him for his support but could tell from the hollow sound of the last few words that he had already severed our connection. Overjoyed with his message I immediately arose and headed for the planning table and my anxious friends. My contact with Violet would have to wait till actual bedtime.

As I approached the table I could see four smiling faces. I guess they were reading of my success with the king written all over my face. I repeated almost verbatim the kings words. They were as delighted as I and vowed to follow the cautions the king spoke of. Mateo was not offended by the king's suggestion. Truth be known, he actually agreed and supported the idea.

Back to our planning of stage one, Mario and Diego sat off to the side deciding questions to ask and what phrases I should learn to be convincing. I stayed with Carlos and Mateo as we kicked around ideas over a final cup of coffee. I really wanted to be in touch with Dove of Spring but did not want to put a damper on the group enthusiasm. With the final darkness setting in it was mutually decided rest was necessary.

I wasted no time in returning to my sleeping area endeavoring to contact my Navajo love. I don't know why but our mental connection was not good this night. Probably my fault with my mind still occupied with my playing the king part. I did, however, manage to hear "Good Night MY Love" so soft and sweet. I then let my jungle symphony take me to slumber land.

Up early and making the morning coffee my mind drifted to my beloved Violet. My commitment was genuine and I realized this more so every day. As much as I loved my work here in the Yucatan I longed as much to be with her. I actually believed we could work well together, here or in the desert. That I decided was my next goal. Working together no matter where or what ever the historical theme. Making this decision actually built up my confidence for today's challenge. The challenge of discovering lost history. I do believe our future knowledge depends much on our past understanding. Something a lot of people of today are dismissing without reason. They seem to be living only for their own future. Enough with the soap box preaching I told myself. Get back to the present endeavor of discovering history.

Diego's soft good morning released me from my trance like state. I returned his greeting with a smile.

"**A**nxious for a second meeting with your would be executers ?" he returned with a smile.

"**V**ery funny. I must admit though I was about at my wits end when you guys showed up. That was probably the most frightening experience of my life."

"**W**hat about the time your archeologist friend buried you alive in the mine pit ?" Diego asked smiling.

I smiled back again saying,

"**N**ot even close, my friend, not even close. Remember I had Mr. Blue to guide me. Enough of my almost demise. What have you four planed for me and our meeting with the ancients ?"

"**L**et me fill my coffee mug first, then we can talk.

We had just seated ourselves when Mario had joined us. Anticipating my thoughts he started with,

"**W**e found an ancient robe that should fit you quite nicely. That along with the scepter should convince them of your validity. I will also rehearse a few phrases with you. Carlos also suggested, with your approval of course, that we bring along a few silk pieces to present to them. He feels this should convince them of our sincerity and hopefully allow them to open up a dialogue."

By now Carlos and Mateo had coffee'd up and found their place at the table. Carlos took over the conversation.

"**W**e should try to keep our visit as short as possible. They already know of the king's commitments, so you should have no problem departing when you think the time is right,"

"**Y**ou mean when we think we have gained the information we are seeking," I questioned.

"**E**xactly." was his quick answer.

We strategized a bit longer then had a quick breakfast. The rest of the day was left to Mario and Diego to rehearse me in my role as king. Mario, of course, was concentrating on my phasing certain statements.

It was important that I be as convincing as possible.

"Convincing to them or to me ?" I thought silently.

The statements he prepared for me were basic and simple but if spoken correctly should convey authority with compassion and not the mandatory "You Must" theme. It was up to me to carry it off. The confidence displayed by my friends helped to bolster my own. I dared not let them down. I knew how important this was to them.

We continued rehearsal, at least my rehearsal, another day before we set off on our mission. The others resumed their paperwork while I was left at camp to practice my king role, which of course, made me chief cook and bottle washer for the day. I didn't mind though, it was still a necessary part of the team work.

As hesitant as I was at playing the part of king I was also excited at the prospect of learning more history; living ancient history.

"Your efforts will again be rewarded Eric."

Not shaken by the king's sudden outreach I could also tell a reply was not necessary. The short message itself had a calming effect on me, yet added to the excitement of our quest.

The rest of the day and evening was routine for all ending with a quiet dinner and early bedtime.

My acting introduction still occupied my mind as I drifted off to sleep totally neglecting to contact Violet.

Chapter 21

The kings entourage left after an early breakfast. As planned Mario was the leader with Diego a few steps behind. I was ten feet or so trailing. Some thirty yards behind were Carlos and Mateo walking quietly and as inconspicuous as possible. Within two hours we sighted the ancient settlement. I could feel myself growing tense.

"Relax Eric. A chosen one does not lack confidence,"

The kings quick words produced the desired effect. I instantly calmed down and took the king's persona.

The noise of moving underbrush alerted us to the presence of others. Six men showed themselves. Three again had lances carrying the Spanish armament. They started to surround Mario and Diego but upon sighting me retreated to a parallel position. I did not look at them but made a mumbled sound directed at Mario. He forged on without hesitation. We were followed by our armed guard.

We entered the large gathering area and stopped just shy of the largest pyramid. Mario turned to me and bowed asking my permission and instructions. I answered almost in a whisper keeping my kingly poise.

Mario waited a few moments for the curious gathering to collect, then in a strong but quiet voice asked for the ruler of this settlement.

Two of the curiosity seekers took off in a run around the pyramid. I , in the meantime, slowly made my way to the alter area. The crowd, without hesitation parted, clearing a pathway for me. All cast their eyes down with a slight bow as I passed. I stopped just shy of the sacrificial alter but remained with my back to the crowd. Thoughts of my last visit here started to enter my head making me uncomfortable.

"This time you have no need to worry my friend. Trust me."

It felt good knowing I was being watched over and I instantly relaxed.

In about three or four minutes the two messenger runners reappeared followed by their almost running leader. One glance and Mario could tell this man was in a very agitated state. He approached Mario and Diego grunting words I obviously did not understand. Mario tried explaining this visit but the overwrought leader appeared to ignore him.

Unobserved by this ruler I slowly turned to see this verbal altercation. At this point the irate ruler raised his scepter to point it at Mario. Diego moved to intercede which garnered the attention of the aggressive man. Ever so slowly I moved to the group. My movement finally demanded attention. A shock and surprised look covered his face. Actually it was now a serious look. As I carefully un- cradled my scepter from my arm fright took over his expression. I quietly uttered one word, "Cease", while at the same time turned pointing the scepter in his direction. He retreated a few steps while completely lowering his own. I halted and re-cradled mine.

Obviously he knew of, or heard of, the power of my scepter I thought.

By now Mario was smiling. Apparently I played my part well. It surprised me also because that was not rehearsed. I slowly turned away walking towards the smaller pyramid, the gathering spectators giving way to my path lowering their eyes and bowing their heads. I in turn also bowed my head slightly acknowledging their respect. To the shy children hiding behind the adults I gave a slight smile. After all children are children no matter where you are or what age you are in.

So far our little charade appeared to be working.

In the meantime Mario and Diego were involved in discussions with several groups with Diego displaying a few silks we brought. The leader took a position off to the side once again but kept his presence nearby to remind the others of his importance. After some discussion their were positive nods of some of the heads. Runners left the group returning within minutes with matching silks.

I pretended to ignore the activities yet kept an eye on the group to gauge the reactions. I would have loved to be involved but understood the sensitivity of the purpose of this mission.

Mario was smiling with a lot of head nodding. Diego also appeared to be pleased with the proceedings. Of course most of the verbal exchange was conducted by Mario.

I continued my supposed inspection of the settlement with as little interaction as possible though I did have a few young ones following me as inconspicuously as possible.

From time to time I would glance towards Mario and Diego. Mario was comfortably sitting with a group appearing to be having a serious discussion, along with smiles and affirmative head nods though I did not know the topic. There was even the occasional arm pointing toward the west from a smiling face.

Diego seemed to be having the same success with his group.   There appeared to be agreement now and then .

From what I could see they lived a simple and not uncomfortable life. From the appearance of the midden heaps * I would say they ate well. I did not glean any evidence of malnutrition in either adult or child. I was fascinated with my little inspection of the ancient past yet I still harbored a slight guilt by our little ruse.

On display under a small overhang of the pyramid, almost like a museum, were various pieces of clothing and armament from the not so welcome Spanish intruders of hundreds of years ago.

Trying not to be noticed the feather adorned ruler was slowly moving closer to the discussion group. But this time bearing a much relaxed facial expression. He was even nodding what appeared to be approval of what was taking place.

* A rubbish pile, sort of like a garbage disposal.

I tried to enccurage the children closer but to no avail. It was not from fear but of respect for the "Chosen One." I pushed no further so as not to undo their teachings. I wanted to leave these people totally undisturbed.

As I moved closer to Mario he caught sight of me and gave me a nod undetectable to those surrounding him. I continued my path to the comfortable gathering and uttered my rehearsed words.

"It is time my son.". Of course I repeated this in the tongue of those unspoiled people.

Both Mario and Diego arose and bowed slightly in my direction. Now the total gathering faced me and bowed. With my right hand I waved them up and politely smiled a loving smile of a king to his people. Mario and Diego joined my side as I again raised my hand.

"Peace and long life my friends." I exclaimed.

Not waiting for acknowledgment I turned to the forest. Mario took his place in front of me with Diego taking up the rear. None of us looked back as we were engulfed by the growth of the jungle. Not a word was spoken by the three of us and we just kept walking knowing Mateo and Carlos were secretly watching our departure just in case. As we surmised there was no attempt to track us.

By design we took a heading ninety degrees to our camp to be on the safe side. We quietly followed this route for just over a half hour before turning to our home base. It was about an hour later when Carlos and Mateo intercepted our pathway. Up till now still not a word was spoken.

Chapter 22

We continued our silent march, our curiosity building all the while about the success or not of our fact finding mission. Again the quiet march on purpose in case we were being trailed. Another hour and a quarter put us at home.

Suddenly I was being congratulated with words and back slapping. I tried to interject my own feelings that it was a joint mission but to no avail. We finally settled down around the coffee pot with all in a finally relaxed breathing state.

Diego was the first to state what was on every body's mind.

"I think that was the biggest thrill of my life, actually being part of life as it was hundreds of years ago."

Carlos, forever the serious professional hurriedly asked
"Well ?"

Mario, all smiles, answered a quick,

"Yes" pausing here just made Carlos more anxious.

"Yes, it was a success. I believe I even learned more than we set out for. What about you Diego ?"

"You are absolutely right. I could not converse as well as you but was making myself understood just fine."

"What about the silks and the Chinese connection ?" was the next anxious question from Carlos.

Mario smiled again.

" They treated this question as matter of fact. They even thought it was odd that I was asking about such a thing. They gave me a sort of "where have you been ?" look. They accepted the silks we offered and even produced some samples of their own which were of the same quality and design."

Here Diego interrupted,

"They spoke to me of the odd looking short men with the funny eyes who told of sailing from far away to the west. Apparently there had been a few visits over a period of years. In turn for the silks they accepted jade and gold trinkets."

Here Mario regained the conversation lead again.

"That was also discussed by the group I was with. Evidently the jade here is slightly different than that in China. Not a greater value, just different. I did not pursue that any further. They also, though briefly, made reference to a female Goddess that appeared from the eastern waters. They revered her as a Goddess because of the shape of her head. They say she must have been of their distant heritage."

"Did you mention our "Golden Lady" ?" asked Mateo

"No. I purposely did not. Why open up trouble."

"That never came up with my group," stated Diego. "But I would not have volunteered that info anyway for the same reason."

Mario continued,

"Their reference to the Goddess is only from oral history stories. Apparently this occurred before their time, long before. All they really know was that she came from the rising sun and a land on the other side of the eastern water. From the land of Quetzalcoatl.** That is why they considered her a God. They did not appear to know of any direct connection between the two."

"Perhaps there wasn't," added Carlos. "They were probably two very distinct yet different periods of history. Our new rewritten history," he added with a smile.

"But it does give us another avenue of history we can add to the mix," added Mateo. "Even if it isn't accepted. At least we five know the truth."

We all smiled and agreed with him.

Not to put a damper on our successful day I interjected.

** The Plumed serpent or feathered serpent God.

"But I personally don't think we should visit them again. Let them live in peace and harmony with nature. Eventually they will probably be found out and there will be the destruction of more valued history. I don't think mankind will ever learn to not destroy our past."

This did put a damper on the up mood of our little camp. When I realized I was doing my thinking out loud I instantly apologized.

"Sorry guys. I do get carried away sometimes."

They accepted my apology and admitted they agreed with me.

Diego lightened the mood by his statement directed at me.

"Are you sure you don't have any more Cognac left. We should really be celebrating."

Mateo joined with,

"Yeah, you should make that three bottles each that you owe us."

I looked at them all and promised.

"Okay, you got it. Unfortunately you'll have to wait a bit. There don't appear to be any liquor stores hereabouts."

Back to a lighter side again the conversation now focused on me and my portrayal of the king.

"Your quick thinking and action with the scepter really saved our whole day," Said Mario. "We could have lost everything because of that "full of himself" leader."

"Yes I knew I was taking a chance, but thinking ahead, I figured if he really knew anything about the king's Scepter he would think twice before asserting himself again."

"You justified to Mateo and I that your wandering about the settlement was also good "PR." Did you learn anything special ?" quizzed Carlos.

"As a matter of fact, I did. Nothing spectacular but sort of an insight to every day life. They apparently ate fairly well. There were some small farm plots slightly off into the jungle. I could not discern exactly what was growing. Their midden heaps also contained various bones. Again I was not close enough to be specific. The children were quite healthy looking with curious eyes and minds. To me all appeared to be perfectly normal for their environment.

Oh yes, I almost forgot. In a corner of the smaller pyramid they had carefully preserved various clothing and armament items as reminders of the Spanish invaders. The general populace did, however, appear to be content. Both men and women. It was only that leader or high priest that was high and mighty."

Eric's four companions all smiled at his ending remark, none of them in disagreement.

"**G**reat observations," answered Carlos. "All the more reason we should leave them undisturbed."

Then to no one in particular he went on almost in a mumble, "I wonder what other history has been lost world wide because of unwanted intervention by a few ignorant people.

No one questioned his remark but all smiled inwardly agreeing with his feelings.

A light discussion continued over the next half hour with nothing new to reveal. We all seemed satisfied with the history we gathered today with out too much disruption to the life of these innocent ancients.

I excused myself from the group and went straight to my hammock. I had much to tell Dove of Spring and was extremely anxious to hear her voice again. That is if I didn't fall asleep first.

At last in a prone position I could feel the tension in my body slowly ease. A few deep breaths and I felt ready to talk to my love. But that was not to be. At least not yet.

"You did well today my friend, as I expected you would."

I hesitated before answering, my thoughts on Violet.

"I see you have other thoughts on your mind and that is also a good thing. We will talk tomorrow Eric."

The fade away was obvious as I smiled to myself. I was

acting like a silly child because I was so anxious to make contact with my heartache.

Now trying to get serious with myself I cleared my head and concentrated on Dove of Spring. Luckily it was not too late and within a minute I heard the smile of her voice.

"I am happy for your success my love. I can feel it in your thoughts."

She startled me with her insight to my mind. She was becoming practiced in our mental connection. I'm sure Whispering Wind has been helping.

I quickly reviewed my days excitement and discovery. I could feel her genuine happiness for me. We mutually pledged our love and commitment each to the other and our longing to be together again.

The jungle symphony filled the gap left by our broken connection. I could not wait for the rainy season that would end our research here. I could already see my travel details back to my Navajo love. I closed my eyes and drifted into blissful repose of total contentment.

Chapter 23

We were all awakened at the same time thanks to our penthouse abiding monkey friends. No matter though, we were all in easy and relaxed moods after yesterdays success. After the coffee was made we happily joined together at the table just enjoying the refreshing morning. I started the conversation inquiring what was in store for today's research. I received no answer. Surprised, I looked carefully at the faces of my four companions. I saw nothing but smiles. My confused expression must have been obvious to all. Now there were even a few laughs.

"Oh, I get it," I smartly remarked. "It's my turn in the hot seat again, is that it ?"

The smiles grew broader confusing me even more. Mario finally came to my rescue explaining that last night after I turned in early they mutually decided to take a day off each to his own liking. Understanding now I joined their smiles.

"Not a bad idea." I agreed whole heartily, my mind instantly going to the "Golden Lady." A more thorough study of her photographically for further research would suit me just fine. I would be able to do exactly what I wanted with out being rushed.

It became obvious to the others that I had drifted into my own world. When I refocused on the present I found myself alone at the table. The others were fixing breakfast including mine.

Slightly embarrassed I put forth my plans for the day off. There were no objections, in fact they were even encouraging me to pursue my craft.

Over our morning meal, day off desires came to light. Diego, as expected, was to take sketch pad in hand and wander. Mario wanted to stay in camp and just relax, possibly catch up on journal entries. Mateo and Carlos were resigned to just doing nothing. Perhaps staying in their hammocks all day. Breakfast over, cleanup shared and we all went our separate ways.

Chapter 24

Having already made numerous visits to this trapezoical structure the trail was easy traveling. Just as well, I was really not in the mood for machete slashing today. Before I knew it I was at the site housing our "Golden Lady".

I decided to walk the perimeter once again still mystified by the four construction styles for the different sides. I still wondered if it was a competition of sorts. No matter, I knew that was an answer I would never know.

Enough of guessing at something that occurred eons ago. It was time to visit the Special Lady.

As I rounded the corner I saw two men approaching. Instantly my guard went up. I continued walking toward them. They were not locals or even from the Yucatan area. The attire appeared to be American. One of them called out a greeting.

"Hello there, perhaps you are the one we are looking for ?"

The voice was definitely American. As we drew closer I could see both men were smiling. They both showed back packs but not very large ones. One had a machete while the other sported a military style automatic pistol in a holster slung low as if in the old West. A tiny alarm went off in my head but I decided to play it cool awaiting further information.

"If you're looking for a hotel, I'm afraid you're a little lost," I quipped.

The men laughed at my light humor and joked back about

taking a wrong turn.

"Are you with the Frank Thurber team."

That flag went up again. I paused before answering.

"I guess you haven't heard. Frank Thurber passed away over a year ago," I said coldly.

"Oh yeah,–ah – we -ah- knew that, but the research team is still going under his name I believe. At least that's what they told us at the Department of Antiquities office."

"There could be some truth in that, but I'm, not buying that yet." I thought.

The one doing the talking stuck out his hand saying,

"Don't mind the dirt. My name is Bill Hudson and this is Tom Warren" pointing to his partner.

I politely answered, "Eric Dexter".

Bill continued on as if we were old friends.

"We're here as an inquiry team for the Smithsonian Institute."

I'm glad I was not by the not so hidden entrance to the "Golden Lady's" house. At least it doesn't look like they detected anything yet.

"It seems the Smithsonian people got the word from the University of Pittsburgh people of your find of a new city. Naturally they are curious as to its authenticity, hence, here we are."

"Oh it's authentic alright. So much so that it could rewrite some history books."

I said that rather challengingly. It wasn't till after I said it I realized I was giving too much information. After silently chastising myself I added,

"At least this is our feeling."

"That's what we are here to study. This, of course, is strictly up to your team," answered Bill quickly

I got the feeling he was back peddling a bit. Again the flag. I know for a fact the Smithsonian people would not do that without a full inquiry stateside of those making the claim of such a find. And even then it would be years before such an expedition would be launched.

"I was just heading back to camp and the others. Join me

and see for yourself , " I said cheerfully.

"Sounds great, we are a bit weary and could use a rest." Bill said smiling.

"So much for my day alone with the Special Lady." I thought.

I slowly made my way back to camp followed by the two strangers. I was purposely going slow so I could send mental warnings to my comrades. I was counting on them to not be too relaxed and not paying attention to our mental telephone.

" *A wise move my young friend, we will talk later."*

The kings voice did not startle me. I was sort of expecting it. It also reenforced my own quick judgement.

It was almost ten minutes before I received a reply from Mario. He said they would all be ready. I felt more comfortable now and picked up the pace a little. There was a light banter of no real consequence on the remainder of our trek. All was friendly.

Finally arriving at home base my four companions played their parts well. They truly acted surprised and welcomed the strangers with hand shakes. I could tell by the facial expressions of the unwanted guests that they were confident in their ruse. Water and snacks were offered and accepted graciously. With all seated at the table I excused myself to put away my camera and equipment. Mateo offered to help and I accepted figuring he had other motives since I only had two things.

"Where did you dig up these two creatures ?" He asked once out of hearing distance.

Surprised at his candor I told him they found me at the Queens tomb. He instantly took on a guarded look.

"Not to worry my friend, I had yet to enter nor was I near any of the entrances."

Relief quickly followed in his eyes.

"They don't know me but I have seen them before and have been warned about them."

Now my mood grew serious. Perhaps my first impression was correct.

"They are treasure seekers, big time. Okay lets get back to the group, I'll give the warning to the others."

On the return to the table Mateo stated.

"Smile now oh "Chosen One.""

His joking worked as I started to laugh. He joined me in the laughter. We looked all innocent as we approached.

Carlos and Mario were at the map table with our guests basically showing the breadth of our new found city. The strangers were playing their parts well as if they were really interested in the history of the Maya. It dawned on me they may very well have had some archeological training but chose the treasure seeking instead.

Diego's mental exchange agreed with my guess. We slyly grinned at each other.

Later in the day they accepted our invitation to stay for dinner and overnight. We tried to make it known that we were too busy to interrupt our schedule of things to accomplish before the rains began. They chose not to push us too much.

"At least for now," I thought.

Again, to me they appeared to be practiced and shrewd about their sleuthing charade.

The night went well, as we expected. But to be on the safe side we five took turns staying awake to keep watch. We were surprised that not one attempt was made to look into the kings tomb during the night. We were not against them seeing the tomb knowing that they could not get to see any of the secret places.

We shared our breakfast willingly so as not to create suspicion in our visitors. While enjoying our coffee and fruit we made our day's plans as was usual. Diego and Mario would show our guests some of the stela we had discovered. This would take them away from camp for a while allowing Mateo time to go to Colonel Rameriz, hoping he would be at the same encampment site, and report our feelings.

Late afternoon the four jungle walkers returned, our guests still playing their parts well acting as if they were totally interested in what they were shown. Carlos then took it upon himself to treat our not so welcome visitors with a prolonged view and discussion of the breadth of our new city discovery at the map table.

Mario and I worked at preparing dinner yet kept an eye on our phony Smithsonian people.

Just before dinner Mateo returned quietly paper work in hand completing his ruse. He mentally reported to us all of his success in contacting Colonel Rameriz. We would probably see him very soon.

In the meantime during our dinner and performing our daily debriefing Bill Hudson, the lead spokesman for our two visitors, asked about the large pyramid behind us. He attempted this in all innocense of course. Carlos chose to answer.

"Of course we've been into it. A few times in fact. It's quite beautiful inside, that is as far as tombs go." He said this straight faced. "Tell you what, since you appear interested we'll give you a tour in the morning. But we must continue our regular work schedule. You never know when the rains are going to start"

"We understand about your paper work. That's why we both were glad for this opportunity to get away from the routine stuff for a while," answered Bill on an up note.

"These guys are really convincing and well practiced." I thought.

"Your observations are well founded my young friend. You were wise to have caught on so fast. They are not here to preserve our history. They have only studied enough to convince those whose heart is not like yours. You and your friends have the situation well in hand. I will be here if you need me."

As was the habit the words echoed away. I smiled hiding it as best I could manage. It did not go undetected by Mario whose words flowed into my head.

"I assume you just heard from the king ?" he asked.

I nodded my head in answer and returned my attention to Carlos describing the inside of the tomb. You could tell the newcomers were more than anxious to get inside. Boy, are they going to be disappointed.

Finally, with the play acting put aside, all seven of us turned in for the night. Again we took turns watching, unobserved, through the night. My turn was not until the wee hours of the morning. This gave me adequate time for a visit with Violet and then my symphony for sleep.

Carlos was up early and after making sure our special guests were asleep he went to the tomb and unlocked the door. None of us wanted them to see the unlocking mechanism which may just tempt them further.

I was also up early and joined Carlos at the coffee pot. We spoke softly not wanting to be overheard. We agreed to down play the tomb and pretend that our main interest was the overall size of this new city complex.

I opened up a little more about my feelings of these two men.

"I know enough about the Smithsonian to know they would not send two investigators to the Yucatan based only on one report of new findings even though they were from reputable people. They would usually require more substantial and positive evidence."

"I can't say that I disagree with you. You are absolutely right. I have had my own dealings with them. Very successful ones I might add," replied Carlos.

"This telepathy thing you learned from the king sure does come in handy. I think that gives us one up on our uninvited Smithsonian reps."

We both laughed quietly.

Soon we were joined by the others including Bill and Tom. Carlos engaged them both in instant conversation about the tomb visit which garnered their immediate attention. I then mentally spoke to the others of my earlier words with him. I received nods of recognition from all.

"Two can play at this game of charades," I thought.

Breakfast went as expected with our guests chomping at the bit to get to the tomb. Carlos played on this masterfully and dragged out the table talk. It was obvious this was really getting to the two men but they held the anxiety quite well.

It was well after nine O'clock when Carlos along with Mario led the pair to the kings tomb. At the last minute I decided to join them curious to see the strangers reaction.

Once at the pyramid Carlos entered followed by Bill and Tom with Mario trailing. I purposely waited for a minute before I joined them. I held a position to allow me a view of both the make believe Reps. I truly wanted to watch their eyes and faces as they viewed the inside. It was obvious, to me anyway, that they had a preplanned scenario. One would look at and talk with Carlos as he pointed out the various sights. The other, in the meantime, cast his eyes about taking in every detail he could. Certain wall spots received extra special attention.

"These gentlemen were well versed in their art, " I thought. *"No wonder they appeared to be so confident."*

"You do well in keeping a close eye on these two."

I heard the king say and fade away as suddenly as it came.

The pair took turns keeping Carlos and Mario engaged in unnecessary questions while the other silently memorized the interior of the tomb.

I went about the job of caretaker by picking up twigs and leaves blown or carried in by us. I know my ruse was working by the expressions exchanged by the two outsiders. They were viewing me just as I wanted them to. A porter or assistant to the other four archeologist scientists.

I received a nod from Mario letting me know of their departure. I acknowledged his signal just as Carlos was winding up his tour much to the disappointment of the guests. They pushed gently for more but Carlos held steadfast repeating how short their time was before the rains and how much was yet to be accomplished. We all exited heading back to the map table area. Our two curious guests kept looking back to the tomb entrance exchanging smiles.

Back at camp both Mario and Carlos held the attention of our guests with their backs to the tomb while Mateo silently closed and secured the lock to the pyramid and quickly allowing himself to be swallowed by the jungle reentering from another direction.

Bill and Tom were asked if they wanted to join in with some of the recording work that we would be doing today. An overanxious refusal was instantly given by Bill.

"**N**o thanks, we don't want to be in your way with that all important work. We thought, that is if you don't mind, we would just wander about the area looking at the interesting structures you pointed out to us on the map."

Carlos hesitated for a moment not liking the idea of them loose on their own, but instantly changed his mind knowing we would all be watching one way or another. The okay from Carlos obviously more than pleased the visitors. Their lack of subtlety of their smiles gave them away which apparently they did not realize.

Carlos, Mario and Diego, after grabbing their note books, left camp in three different directions. This left Mateo and I alone with the phonys. They fussed about for fifteen minutes or so till Bill anxiously asked.

"**A**re you two not going to do your recording work ?"

Mateo happily volunteered that it was his day to stay in camp and work on lunch and dinner and catch up on his journal work.

Disappointment instantly showed in our guest. They then turned to me with questioning eyes. I, like Mateo, quickly volunteered that I still had photographic work to catch up on and would most likely be gone all day.

In order to cover their instant pleasure of my answer Tom asked,

"**I**s there anything we can help you with ?"

"**I** wish there was," I answered. "But this is strictly a one man job." I finished with a broad grin. "I just have to gather up my equipment and I'll be on my way."

"You never saw two happier people," I thought. *"I believe they thought they had their way now."*

Mateo went about doing chores, just about ignoring Bill and Tom. They played it cool for a while hanging around the map table. Finally they made their move and ever so slowly drifted towards the kings tomb. It was a lot of fun watching them arrive only to find no entrance way. Trying to look innocent they did everything they could to open the stone door.

They stood aside and were discussing their frustration with serious and intense faces. Obviously coming to a decision they returned to the camp area where Mateo was updating his journal.

Talking with Mateo after the fact, I found out the two men were politely asking about the door to the tomb. That is politely at first. Eventually they turned nasty and began getting physical. Dragging Mateo up from his chair they started pushing him toward the pyramid. They were not being gentle either. Mateo, however, patiently played his part well.

We had no idea they would turn to violence. My thoughts were sent to the others. Carlos answered in short order.

"Mateo knew what might happen and we are all here to intercede should it become necessary. Colonel Ramirez is also here."

I still did not like the idea that Mateo was being physically man handled but felt better with Carlos's words.

"I am here also my friend. Mateo will not be harmed."

I was wondering if the king was witness to these happenings.

Now at the tombs entrance the pair got a little rougher in their man handling. I could hear Mateo trying to explain that he did not know how to open the tomb. Only Carlos knew.

"I guess we grabbed the wrong patsy," laughed Bill. Perhaps a little pain will loosen your tongue."

Just as Bill Hudson was about to draw his pistol Colonel

Rameriz, not dressed in uniform, stepped forward from his green hiding place.

"I would not do that if I were you Sen'or."

Startled by the voice Bill and Tom swung around to see Rameriz and another man, also not in uniform.

"Are you trying to cut in on drug trade Sen'or That is not a very good thing to do. That would make me very unhappy."

Thinking quickly Bill right away spoke out,

"It's not your drugs we are after but we happen to know there is gold and other treasures hidden in this tomb."

"Oh really." answered the colonel. "And because of that you were going to beat my brother. I do not like the games you play Sen'or."

Totally taken aback by these words Bill instantly tried another tactic.

"Boy ! These guys are well practiced in cunning." I thought.

"Tell you what, help us get into this tomb and we will split the treasure with you and your brother. We will have to work fast before the others return,"

The eyes of Bill and Tom were focused on the Colonel as they saw his face turn ultra serious.

"So now Sen'or you are trying to steal my heritage and my history. Will the world ever leave us alone. First you destroy the books of my history and now you want to continue destroying my heritage. You are not a very nice man Sen'or."

Now in a state of panic Bill blurted out, " OKAY, OK. You can have all the treasure, just let us go about our business."

"I can not do that Sen'or. If I did that I would not be doing my job correctly."

The colonel paused sporting a big smile. During the pause Bill attempted to draw his gun again. Mateo, thinking quickly, grabbed his arm twisting it behind his back.

"Thank you my brother. We can take it from here."

Looking directly at the pair of intruders Rameriz spoke officially.

"You are now under arrest Sen'or."

"What for, and who are you to arrest me," Bill shouted strongly. We have done nothing."

Colonel Rameriz smiled. "To start with Sen'or, physical harassment of this young man. Then attempting theft of National Treasure. Then add to that attempted bribery." He paused again. "And if that is not enough, Here I have a list of eight other charges against you and your cohort."

While speaking the Colonel reached into his pocket for the list of charges.

All was quiet for a moment.

Bill with a very cynical smirk on his lips confidently replied,

"And you, just one man are going to take me back to a civilized town all alone and through the jungle."

Tom was also smiling by now.

"But I am not alone Sen'or. I have friends."

What a few scientists ?" Laughed Bill.

Not liking to be laughed at the colonel with a most serious expression raised his right arm. Out of no where there appeared thirty camo clad men, weapons at the ready.

"Si, me Colonel." said one of the men as a few of the others stepped forward encircling Bill and Tom.

At this point myself and the others appeared again to the surprise of our pair of thugs. In short order our special guests were restrained and taken away. The Colonel remained only a few minutes longer.

"Thank you my friends, we have been after these two for quite some time. They will bother you no longer, I can guarantee that."

I naively spoke again about Mateo being his brother.

"Biologically no Sen'or but all Maya are brothers because of our heritage."

As Colonel Rameriz turned to leave he quickly turned

back to me;

        "**I** still think you look familiar Sen'or Dexter. Are you sure we have not met before ?"

        Smiling he shook my hand and was soon swallowed by the jungle

        We all naturally were concerned for Mateo who in turn assured us he was okay. Then all four ,looking directly at me, said in different ways, "Not to bring home any more strangers who are wandering about the jungle." I knew then all was back to normal.

        The king tuned into all of us.

        "You have done well my friends. You can be proud of your heritage."

        He then quickly faded away.

        We decided another day of relaxation was in order. Diego and I went fishing for dinner while the other three just relaxed.

Chapter 25

The fishing went well and that night we all stuffed ourselves. Of course I took a lot of harassment for not having any more Cognac to top off the evening. The only way to stop the personal annoyance was to promise three bottles each of the special elixir I spoiled them all with.

Finally out from under the verbal assault I started with my own counter attack about their wasting almost two days of lounging around doing nothing productive. I would not accept the fact that they were distracted by two men out to rob the king's tomb.

Of course they immediately turned my accusations around reminding me that it was I who brought them into camp.

By bedtime we all were thoroughly laughed out. Believe it or not we were all actually exhausted from the days lack of physical activity and the evenings silly laughter.

We went to our respective sleeping areas and were happy for the peace of the night. I bid my love and sent good night to Dove of Spring and sank into my hammock. I think I was asleep before I finished zipping up my mosquito netting.

Up early with my mug of black syrup I felt I could now actually concentrate on my day with the "Golden Lady". The others were also seriously returning to their boring, nonetheless, necessary paper work. We all were in good humor and looking forward to a productive day. We chose our five different directions and faded into the jungle.

It didn't take too long to reach the house of the "Golden

Lady". I truly admired this odd shaped structure though still confused by its construction style. I guess that's one answer we will never get. I walked all four sides once again taking in the beauty of this massive undertaking.

We did such a good job of hiding the entrance I almost did not find it. I felt a little foolish yet at the same time satisfied that we did such a good job.

I quietly entered the "Golden Lady's" chamber still astonished at her beauty and majesty. I stood frozen in place for more than five minutes in utter devotion to the magnetic appeal of this golden wonder. I wondered what it must have been like to actually have known her as a living person.

I apologized to her for my lingered staring..

"Listen to me. First I talk to large spiders, then to jungle cats and now to a frozen in time mummy." I must really be losing it, I scolded myself.

Finally putting my head back on straight I set about doing the job I came to do. I photographed the throned lady from every angle possible. I even managed a number of stereo pairs for three dimensional viewing at a later date. All the while I was extremely intrigued. Not just her beauty, but the whole mystery of what she was doing here so far away from her home. History truly has to be rethought. But again that is something that will probably never happen. Man is funny that way. Once something is established no one dares think about changing no matter what new evidence or finds arise.

I remembered the preliminary quick measurements we did after our first discovery of the Special Lady. We are looking at plus or minus seventy five hundred miles by the way the crow flies. And this is when most historians said long distance navigation did not take place. Again, if I remember correctly, traces of Phoenician and Egyptian ships have been found around the east coast of the United States.

I laughed to myself. I find this rather funny. Here I am looking at this wondrous Lady from thousands of years ago, yet history says it was not possible. I guess someone forgot to tell the ones who made the trip.

Then again there is the added mystery of why she came here and why is she the only one here. She could not have come alone.

"Perhaps she took the local airliner," I clowned out loud.

"It is good that you can laugh my friend. It is a true sign that you have both feet firmly planted in facts."

The kings voice startled me. This was one time I really did not expect it. I answered without hesitation,

"Can you enlighten us any. This enigma goes against all normal logic ?"

"Does it really my friend. Your own thoughts of just minutes ago sort of answered your questions. Again, you do not believe even your own logic of mysterious situations. Review all you have seen and include your friends. Chances are your conclusions will be correct. Go by your facts and instinct my friend and you will realize why I believe you are a chosen one. Reflect on your thoughts and you will find them to be correct. The true answers are in your heart and your whole being. Do not discount yourself."

With that statement the king faded away. I made no attempt at additional contact.

I sat there silently reviewing all my conversations with Atl. All he has told me, yet another part of me continues on with doubts of myself.

I sat here for another who knows how long my mind a total blank. I wasn't even thinking. The growl of my stomach pulled me out of my nothing trance. No wonder I was hungry. I had not eaten for over eight hours. Automatically and mindlessly I put away my equipment. I so wanted to protect the film I just exposed of the "Golden Lady".

I hesitated before exiting the throne room. Looking at the all perfect face I spoke out loud,

"Perhaps you have answers for me my queen. Right now I can use all the encouragement I can find."

I held eye contact with her for quite a while not really expecting any thing. At last deciding to start my return to camp I felt a tingle run through me. It was the same tingle I felt with the jungle cat on my way here a few weeks ago. I shook my head to clear it and turned again to the Lady. A tingle eased it's way through me again. I did not want to believe this was happening. This was getting weird now.

Like a silly child I said "Good bye My Lady" and walked briskly to the exit. I made sure all was locked and the outside entrance well hidden again. I was proud of myself in the way I made it disappear.

I took off at a good gait for camp, food and rest.

~ ~ ~ ~ ~ ~

I arrived just before total darkness. I entered our home area apologizing knowing my friends were concerned. I assured them all was Okay and that I just got carried away with my photographing of the Lady. Diego helped lessen the tension by clowning his usual way.

"Stick to your Navajo maiden, at least she's still breathing."

We all chuckled over his remark. I couldn't even think of a decent reply. He caught me completely off guard..

Lucky for me they did save some dinner for me.

We all discussed our day while I ate. Shortly after satisfying my stomach I headed for my hammock and sleep. I barely finished zipping the netting and I was out for the night.

Chapter 26

I was feeling refreshed from a good nights rest but still troubled by something I just could not put my finger on. Carlos and I met at the coffee pot at the same time.

He appeared to be pre - occupied with the still misty rain.

We flipped to see who would make the morning brew. Carlos smiled as he sat down saying,

"You make it better than the rest of us anyhow."

While waiting for the dark syrup I reviewed yesterday with him. When speaking of the "Golden Lady" my unknown nagging made itself known. It was she, the displaced Egyptian Queen or Princess or whatever her title. I quickly mentioned this to Carlos but chose not to go into detail until the others were also present. Carlos being polite as always accepted my decision.

It was not too long when the five of us were at the table enjoying a quick but satisfying breakfast.

"Now that I have every bodies attention, I - - - ."

I was interrupted by Diego's wit.

"Okay, what is it going to cost us this time ?"

Still smiling I replied.

"I don't know yet, I haven't quite figured that out yet."

Before I could get into my yarn the traces of misty rain became a definite soft rain.

"Looks as if our season is nearing its end," said Mario

rhetorically.

We all smiled and shook our heads in agreement.

I continued on using the rain as my introduction.

" This rain, though unwanted, blends in nicely to what I'm about to say, or rather ask."

My opening instantly garnered their attention.

"As you know I spent quite a bit of time yesterday with our "Golden Lady. Certain scenarios kept popping into my mind. Things that I really did not like."

I paused here to gauge reactions. I internally smiled knowing I really had their attention now. Moving on slowly questioning my own reasoning, I finally decided to let out my innermost feelings.

"This is your project, not mine, so the final decision is yours but here are my true feelings."

Here I took a deep breath cleansing my mind, then proceeded nervously.

"The world is not ready for what we have discovered to date. A treasure trove beyond value, an unknown mountain tunnel that goes on for miles, A ventilator system far beyond our present civilizations understanding; an Egyptian connection before it was believed possible; a Chinese connection for trade and knowledge exchange and finally we have our "Golden Lady". It's our "Golden Lady" that I'm concerned about.

Here I paused again to choose my next words. Carlos started to speak. I instantly held up my hand to stop him.

"Please let me finish, I don't know when I'll get this brave again."

He smiled some what and nodded his head.

"I don't want to give up our Egyptian Queen," I stated rather firmly.

There reaction was what I expected. A sort of shocked reaction that I would be so emphatic. I smiled a little to ease the sudden tension.

"I will now outline my reasoning hoping you will not feel too ill of me."

"I think a lot of this was brought about by our recent two

unwanted visitors. They sort of gave me a red flag warning. This hidden city is a great thing for the whole world. It will only help further the study of your Maya culture. There is undeniable proof of the housing, tombs and pyramids, not even mentioning the Stele which validates history, people and dates. The tunnel system speaks for itself. It is a feature to study for future engineering along with the fresh air vent system. Even the Chinese connection, though a bit of a stretch, is or can be a believable situation. The silks prove that. We also have the world wide trade contracts in combination with the Navejo. And I almost forgot the world map and its accuracy far outdating any old maps we have found to date. I'm sure they will also eventually be validated. Even the treasure room with all it's worth will be protected by the government and Department of Antiquities. I'm also sure the Mural Hallway will be a boon to the art world and the real artists of today will not let that be destroyed or compromised in any way."

  I looked directly at Diego as I spoke. His smile and affirmative nod confirmed my own feelings.

  "That being said brings us to the "Golden Lady". How do we present her ? How do we protect her? As we all know there are those out there who would go to unseen lengths to get their hands on that gold. They would not care about the historical significance she represents."

  I hesitated again while I took a deep breath.

  "I'm almost finished. I'm not suggesting we never reveal her presence. Just hold off for a time until we know of protective measures so that the world can appreciate her contribution to history. That structure which has been her home for eons was built with out doors. There must have been a reason for this. True, we found an entrance but we had help."

  "What I'm proposing is that we seal up these portals to make them difficult or impossible to find. At a later date, who knows perhaps years, we can reveal our find knowing by then she will be properly protected. We already have enough finds to turn the Archeological world on its ear, and by our own admission it is going to be a hard sell. And once the news of the "Golden Lady" gets out it is going to be an impossible sell. Except of course the tomb robbers who care nothing about history."

  I paused a third time to catch my breath and calm myself down. None of my friends made any attempt to interject. They were giving me my say.

"So my proposition is to make the entranceway we found to disappear as much as possible. When you four deem it necessary you can then bring her to light to the proper Mexican and world authorities. Whether it's five years, one year or twenty years. At least this way we will be doing all we can to protect her and what she means to world history."

I sat back, a little out of breath.

"That's my story and my true feelings. Nothing I said was meant to offend you."

All was quiet for a spell with my four friends looking at each other and not me.

"I really did it this time," I thought. *"They will never ask me back again. Oh well, I still have my Navajo world."*

Mateo was the first to finally react. Slowly he brought his hands together and quietly started to clap at my performance. I did not know how to react. One by one the other three joined in the applause along with smiles. Carlos, with direct eye contact voiced,

"I could not have put it any better myself."

This statement was echoed by the others. The nervousness and tension now relieved I know I made the right decision.

"Thank you my friends for allowing me to run off at the mouth."

Diego, ever the clown asked,

"Are you sure you're not running for Congress. Speechifying like that will get you elected."

Of course we all laughed with that. Carlos brought us back to seriousness.

"I think we all in our own way and in our own mind have been tackling the same feelings. You have just put it into words most succinctly."

Mario joined with,

"I believe you are absolutely correct. Who knows what would happen to this Egyptian connection if announced to the world prematurely.

"It seems, my desert wandering friend, we are all in

agreement," stated Mateo. "I know we may not have too much of this season left, what with this heavy mist we are now experiencing. We may not complete all that we came to do but I for one think our "Golden Miss" should have our full attention right now."

Ever so slowly smiles started and all were agreed.

"Then it's settled," spoke Carlos emphatically. "We do what we can for the Lady and if we have time we can go back to our super interesting paper work."

Diego happily interjected,

"But before we end this productive meeting, Eric must give us his word on two things. First, not to discover any more new things in this season. Second, and most important he must promise another bottle of Cognac each. I believe that would make three each if I'm not mistaken."

Four sets of very serious eyes now stared at Eric.

"For the sake of the Queens protection it's worth it, even if it is you four," replied Eric accompanied by a broad smile.

Carlos took his usual lead again.

"Okay ! It appears we are all in agreement of protecting our Egyptian guest. Now the difficult part. The how and when. We know the when is soon because of the rains, which leaves us the how. Personally I think we should all think seriously on this. Let's say for the rest of the day. First order of business tomorrow we all outline our plans of how to make the door disappear."

Here he left it. We all sort of half smiled at each other and left it at that.

Carlos was right though, this was going to take a lot of thought. Let's see how good we can be at hiding things like their ancestors.

~ ~ ~ ~ ~ ~

The rest of our day was just make work stuff. Each of us keeping to ourselves with our own interests. Lunch was an individual thing but dinner was our usual get together and clowning, of course with me the primary butt of all the jokes. We collectively avoided any talk of the Queen. It was truly a relaxing day save for our individual thoughts on protecting the Queen.

Once dinner was cleared we each returned to our sleeping area and let the night take us to our own dreamland.

"I am proud of you my friend. You truly are a chosen one. Your arguments for protecting the Lady from Egypt showed your true heart. I'm sure the five of you will succeed. Let the artist in Diego take the lead on this. You will not be sorry."

The soft echo of the word sorry told me of the Kings departure.

"Just as well." I thought. *"I can always contact him tomorrow if need be."*

The silence of the jungle now left me time for Dove of Spring. Before I could even clear my head her soft voice filled my being with a joy I had not felt in years.

"I am here my love as I always will be."

"It won't be too much longer my flower and we will be together again."

"Your words have now made my world complete. I have a message for you and your friends from Whispering Wind. He says to let the artist among you have his way with your Egyptian guest. His heart is truly suited to the task.

I must go now my love but my heart awaits your presence."

I was not prepared for such a short contact but my efforts to reconnect were fruitless. However Violet's words combined with the tranquility of the jungle filled me with an inner contentment I had never experienced before. My mind seemed to float with the jungle symphony. I was one with the jungle and at peace with the world.

A familiar faint echo brushed past me.

"This is the way of all Chosen Ones."

I was alone again but at peace.

Chapter 27

It was a somber mood this morning. Even at the coffee pot there was very little chatter. I'm sure it was the "Golden Lady" causing the mood. How to protect her being the major thought. At least it was for me.

After a few wake up sips of our coffee Diego spoke out.

"I have a plan that I think will work, but it will take some hard work from all of us together. Even without Cognac."

He ended with looking at me, his usual smile glowing.

"I'm glad someone has some thoughts." replied Carlos. "Everything I came up with I dismissed myself. They were all too obvious, and that's what we are trying to avoid.

Mario and Mateo repeated pretty much the same thing. Now of course every one looked at me.

"Don't look at me, I drew pretty much the same blank also no matter what I thought of. However I did have a short visit from the king and even a shorter message from Whispering Wind, the Navajo elder. Follow Diego's lead."

"I was just getting to that," Diego said with a slight embarrassed grin. "The king paid me a direct visit last night inquiring of my thoughts. When I told him my quick idea he said how pleased he was and that he knew I was the one to do it."

"Well I guess that's settled then. Who are we to go against the king's desires ?" Carlos finalized.

As an after thought Diego mentioned that if he had more time he would duplicate the faux trees of their ancestors. But time we did not have.

After a pause in conversation Mario finally spoke for us all.

"Okay, let's take care of breakfast and then report to the boss for assignments."

Diego laughed along with the rest of us saying,

"Gee, I sort of like being the boss."

Of course that just opened up our harassment slings. For once it was not me on the receiving end.

~ ~ ~ ~

Breakfast was a more relaxed atmosphere compared to our pre breakfast seriousness. The joviality continued through cleanup. We then became professionals again. As was agreed Diego took charge.

"Before I get into any detail I want to preface my statements with a genuine plea. Please allow me to finish my presentation before you walk away and start throwing rocks at me."

He said this with a half smile but you could tell by his eyes that he was quite serious. We all nodded in agreement.

"Okay, first the "Golden Lady's" door. We are going to dig up a tree, roots and all and move it here along with a few large stones. The stones will go on the horizontal door along with some door and miscellaneous shrubbery. For the Chinese door I feel a few well placed rocks, heavy ones, and an assortment of dirt and grasses."

Diego paused to let this sink in before continuing.

"Wait. It gets even more difficult, but personally I believe we can do it. I believe we can accomplish this with a tree about fifteen feet tall. I also think it should come from at least a half mile away for obvious reasons. The stone or rocks we can gather from where ever and make their former resting place disappear quite easily. The tree we leave as a downed tree covering the in ground door again with a few strategically placed rocks. I truly feel confident we can accomplish this in three days or less."

Again a pause. Carlos started to raise his hand but Diego politely cut him off.

"Wait, I'm not finished yet. I realize you are thinking of how do we move these rocks and tree without modern equipment. Well I believe I have the answer for that also. The tree we find we can carry. The type I'm thinking of are very prolific in this part of the jungle. Not only that but they are basically light weight and very easily bow to the wind, and are often uprooted. So another fallen tree does not raise suspicion."

He paused here again and with a half smile added,

"Unless you are Eric."

This of course drew the expected laughter.

"As far as the heavy stones we pick those that are too heavy for one but not for three. And again thanks to Eric we build a skid, as he did to carry my sorry bones out of the tunnel. Only this time we will have a better choice of material."

Here Diego stopped, took a deep breath and sat back in his chair as if exhausted.

"Okay, now you can throw those stones at me." he smiled.

Carlos broke the short silence.

"You know, I think that just might work. I'll have to agree with you. I think we can do that in three days. Perhaps less."

Suddenly all of us were in agreement on both completing the job and in less than three days.

"But !!" Carlos cautioned in a raised voice, "I must reiterate what was mentioned earlier. This will all be possible if Eric agrees not to discover anything new for at least three days."

At last I reclaimed my old position again. The brunt of all jokes.

After we all calmed down from our little "pick on Eric" interlude we turned to Diego for guidance which he was ready to give. He apparently worked on this plan all night and put a lot of himself into the logistics of this plan.

"I believe the tree should be our first priority. That will take all five of us. Not that it's that heavy but it will make the digging much easier."

Mateo questioned Diego's statement.

"Can't we just pull it down ?"

"Not if we want it to look like it uprooted itself. We have to dig at least two to three feet all around to maintain the root ball." replied

Diego casually.

"You really have thought this out." added Mario.

Diego just humbly smiled.

I asked the obvious question.

"When can we start ?"

It was answered by Carlos.

"Personally I think we should start on the tree tomorrow since about half of today has already passed. We can spend the rest of today working on the skids necessary right here at camp."

Diego smiled his approval.

I thought to myself;

"A half day at home base would be great for moral though our comradery was at a point already that it could not be beat. "

We all turned to finding what we thought would be the best material to make the skids necessary to move the rock needed. It was hard work but physically only. We were actually enjoying ourselves. Of course all of this was the joking about the skid I made to carry Diego out of the tunnel. I did not have the resources we now enjoyed but it did the job. As the old saying goes "Necessity is the mother of all invention."

~ ~ ~ ~ ~ ~

We became so involved in the skids we by passed lunch. No one seemed to care though.. By days end we had two working skids and we were confident they would be more than adequate for the task.

Late afternoon found us relaxing at the dinner table with large water cups discussing what to do about dinner. It was decided by all, except me, that Eric take care of dinner preparations because it was my idea to hide the "Golden Lady" and because of that they had to do this extra physical work. I agreed willingly which took the wind out of their "Pick on Eric" sails. And so ended our day.

Chapter   28

It's amazing how cooperation works. With all five of us together we had the tree dug up and moved and in place at the trapezoidal structure in just over six hours. With some finishing touches it looked quite natural and hid well the Queens entranceway. We felt good about our accomplishment and headed home for a relaxing supper knowing we could finish the rock moving tomorrow and so end the task of protecting the "Golden Lady".

The balance of the day was spent resting along with journal updating. We all succumbed to the symphony of the jungle and turned in early for a good nights rest.

I made my report to Dove of Spring and let the music drift me to sleep.

The up and moving mode continued in all of us and by mid day the silk room door was also well hidden. Pleased with our disappearing act we headed for home base and an afternoon of fishing for dinner.

The misty rain was back again which told us our season was nearing its end. All appeared to view this with mixed emotions. Sorry to see our research ending but glad to head home away from the oppressive heat, the biting bugs and of course our howler monkey friends. Our screeching friends will probably have a celebration party when we leave.

~ ~ ~ ~ ~ ~

The next two weeks we worked at whatever we could between the intermittent rains which seemed to be getting heavier by the day. Slowly, piece by piece, we dismantled our camp storing many items in the kings tomb knowing they would be back next season. In fact we even slept in the tomb the last few nights due to the sudden downpours that occurred at night.

We tried reading the sky as best we could hoping to coordinate our leaving time so that we were not trudging through the rain drenched jungle when we started home.

Luck was with us for a change. Our water taxi was waiting for us when we arrived at the river. The ride back to Oxaca was pleasant but wet. It's amazing how the jungle canopy acts as an umbrella shielding us from the rain. The river was lacking that protective cover. We were not bothered that much by the drenching rain because we knew we were heading home.

After Oxaca was Mexico City where we caught our flights, my colleagues to Arizona and I to my waiting Navajo love.

Perhaps Diego was right. Returning to my living, breathing Navajo queen was more comfortable than the Egyptian "Golden Lady".

Children's Stories

(Ten adventures with Squiggy the Squirrel)

1- The Garden Mystery

2- The Christmas Garland Mystery

3- The New Land

4- New Friends

5- Squiggy and the Bear

6- Squiggy and the Storm

7- The Next Generation

8- Squiggy's Main Vacation

9- Squiggy and the Virus

10- Suzette Squirrel